Abby—California Gold

BOOK 3 IN ABBY'S SOUTH SEAS ADVENTURES SERIES

DON'T MISS THE OTHER EXCITING TITLES!
#1 *Lost at Sea*
#2 *Quest for Treasure*
#4 *Secret at Cutter Grove*

SOUTH SEAS ADVENTURES

Abby
California
Gold

PAMELA WALLS

TYNDALE
KIDS

TYNDALE HOUSE PUBLISHERS, INC.
WHEATON, ILLINOIS

Visit the exciting Web site for kids at www.cool2read.com
and the Abby Web site at www.abbyadventures.com

Interior map: Gold Rush Album by Joseph Henry Jackson, Charles
Scribner's Sons, Copyright © 1949. Reprinted by permission of The Gale
Group.

Scripture quotations are taken from the *Holy Bible,* New International
Version®. NIV®. Copyright © 1973, 1978, 1984 by International Bible
Society. Used by permission of Zondervan Publishing House. All rights
reserved.

ISBN 0-8423-3628-1, mass paper

Printed in the United States of America

08 07 06 05 04 03 02 01
10   9   8   7   6   5   4   3   2

To Debbie and Gray Judge,
friends for life.
Thanks for your abiding love and faith.

The Almighty will be your gold,
the choicest silver for you.
Job 22:25

Acknowledgments

A SPECIAL THANKS TO JUNE CROWE, MY MOM,
WHO TOOK US ON OUR OWN GOLDFIELD ADVENTURE,
AND TO AN EDITOR WORTH HER WEIGHT IN CALIFORNIA
GOLD—RAMONA CRAMER TUCKER.

Chapter One

APRIL 1848

Abby Kendall bent over the blank page of her
tattered journal, pencil poised. For a moment her
mind traveled back three weeks to the day she and
her younger sister, Sarah, had left their family in
Hawaii and begun their sail to California. Having
crossed the ocean, they were now skimming along
the California coast. Absently Abby twisted a ringlet
with one hand as her vivid blue eyes stared unseeing
at the page. She barely noticed the pitch and roll of
the ship as the heartbreaking scene unfolded in her
mind one more time.

"Take good care of your sister," Pa had ordered
as he stood in the sand at the ocean's edge just
before they were rowed from the island of Oahu
to the waiting ship. Abby could see him swallow
hard, as if he was having a hard time letting them
go. "Obey Luke's aunt. She's a stern woman, but
I know she'll help us out until your ma gets better.
And she has a lot of servants, so you'll be well taken
care of."

Abby's stomach twisted as she remembered how her temper had flared. "But Pa, Sarah and I can stay here and help you take care of Ma! We'll live in the barn so we don't catch the fever—and I'll-I'll do all the cooking over a campfire for you. For goodness' sake, Pa, I'm thirteen years old!"

Thomas Kendall had raked his big knuckles through his wavy hair. The look of distress on his face as Sarah clung to his waist made Abby regret her words. "We've been through this, Abby. Your ma wants you and Sarah away from her illness. We're not sure what it is, and she can't bear the thought of you catching it. It's important we don't worry her. As soon as Ma's better, we'll write you."

Abby chewed her lip. *Pa doesn't trust me to take care of Sarah, or cook meals, or do all the things I know I can do!* The terrible thought plagued her. And worst of all, Pa had sent her away when Ma needed her most.

Abby remembered peering through her parents' bedroom window on Uncle Samuel's ranch to see Ma lying still on the bed. Her mink-brown hair was sweaty, her fevered cheeks an unnatural crimson.

Abby now raised her eyes to the swinging oil lamp near her cabin door.

What if Ma dies—and I never see her again? Her chest tight with anxiety, she put the pencil to the paper and began to write.

2 April 1848

Dear God,

  My heart's gripped in worry. It's been almost a month since we left, and our ship has finally sailed into San Francisco Bay. But all I want to know is, Did Uncle Samuel bring a doctor from Honolulu? Surely a doctor came to Kailua to help Ma two weeks ago. But Uncle Samuel said it could take time. What if the doctor was gone on rounds in the countryside, or what if he wouldn't travel all those miles to the other side of the island? How I wish there was a doctor on our side of the island!

Abby paused, listening to the sounds of sailors' feet hurrying on the deck above her. They had probably entered San Francisco Bay, but the bay water was choppy and rough, making writing hard. She bent back to the page.

  When Luke and I went on our Lanai treasure hunt and found that bag of gold and silver coins, I thought all our troubles were over. But it wasn't enough money! Most of it had to be spent to search for a doctor for Ma, so there wasn't enough to buy the ranch. And we had to use some to travel. Only You and I know how much Ma wants a place of her own, a place to call home. I sure want Ma to have that someday.

Suddenly, a loud metallic crashing echoed through the hull of the ship as the anchor chain played out and splashed into the sea. Abby dashed off a final thought.

> *It's time to disembark. I wonder what lies ahead at Mrs. Gronen's mansion. I guess we'll soon find out.*

She slammed the journal shut and hid it in her satchel on the bunk just as eight-year-old Sarah, dressed in her burgundy wool coat, burst through the door. "Come on, Abby! You can see San Francisco. The fog just blew away, and we're almost home!"

Abby slipped on her blue wool coat and buttoned it. "Home is in Hawaii now, not Pueblo de San Jose."

Sarah looked confused. "But I'll get to see all my friends, right?"

Abby's face softened. It'd been only six months since they'd moved from Pueblo de San Jose, California, to Oahu to help their sick uncle, Samuel, run his ranch. Abby knew that Sarah still felt attached to her old life. "Of course. But first we have to settle in at Mrs. Gronen's. Then we can visit friends."

Sarah's pale-blonde eyebrows rose as she tossed her corn silk hair over her shoulder. "Won't it be fun to show off Kini? He's a real Hawaiian boy—and a hero!"

Abby and Luke had told Sarah stories of their adventure on Lanai and how ten-year-old Kini had helped them escape from an angry *kahuna,* the Hawaiian priest.

As Abby followed Sarah out the door and up the hatch, she thought of Kini with his short-cropped raven hair. His round face and dark-brown eyes were as familiar to her now as Luke's green eyes and sandy hair. Although fourteen-year-old Luke would always be her best friend, Kini was rapidly becoming the younger brother she'd never had.

Abby knew he'd risked everything to set her and Luke free, and he'd paid a price to do it. His grandfather, Mako, had been so furious that Kini had been forced to flee Lanai, too. But when they'd returned to her uncle's ranch in Kailua, Kini had gotten to know her family quickly. He now had a place in the Kendalls' home and heart, just like Luke, who'd been orphaned three years earlier.

Abby's heart brightened as she climbed through the hatch and smelled the briny sea breeze. She remembered how her family had camped together on the beach their first week back in Kailua. Duncan MacIndou, the Scottish investigator who'd been hired to find Luke and return him to his aunt in California, had said they deserved to spend time with her family before sailing back. They had swum and fished and even canoed with her Hawaiian friends.

But when they'd arrived back at the ranch, Ma

had suddenly come down with a mysterious fever. Duncan had offered to fetch the doctor from Honolulu, and Abby recalled the look of gratitude in Pa's eyes. But Uncle Samuel had insisted on going, taking some of the silver coins Abby had found on Lanai.

Overnight Ma's illness had worsened. Pa had moved everyone but himself to the barn and waited three days to make sure no one else had caught it. That's when Abby overheard Pa asking Duncan to escort his children to California. "It's a godsend you're here," Pa said. "We wouldn't feel comfortable sending them off unless they had a trusted chaperon."

Over the past month, Abby had come to trust Duncan, too. His prayers for her mother meant the world to her, for the Scotsman spoke to the Almighty as if he had a direct link to Him.

Now as Abby and Sarah climbed on deck, the cold California wind made Abby shiver. The girls headed toward the bow of the bobbing ship to join the Scottish investigator and the two boys.

Duncan, a black eye patch covering his left eye, turned to greet them. "Ah, 'tis a grand view!" he exclaimed in his Scottish brogue as he twirled his handlebar moustache, a habit that had become familiar to Abby. All around them sailors scurried to take in the sails as the captain shouted orders. Abby could hear the happy excitement in the men's voices.

The sun had broken through the clouds that lay over the coastline, and Abby caught her first glimpse of San Francisco, a small port town of adobe buildings on the hill above the bay.

"Look at all the ships!" Luke exclaimed. His face dimpled with a grin as he pointed at the many sloops, barks, and schooners anchored nearby.

A sailor, coiling a hemp rope, nodded at his words as he viewed the crowded bay. "I've never seen so many here before. I wonder what's brought them."

Kini touched Luke's shoulder, then gestured toward the buildings on shore. "Is Aunt Dagmar's house over there?"

"No," Luke answered. "We'll catch a barge on its way down the bay to Alviso Landing. Then it's a long walk to Pueblo de San Jose, where my aunt lives."

Sarah's eyes sparkled with enthusiasm. "First thing I'm gonna do is climb my tree," she announced.

Kini grinned with anticipation. "Your tree has coconuts?"

She giggled. "No, but it might have apricots pretty soon."

Abby's blue eyes darkened with concern. She knew Sarah didn't understand that there was no going back to their old life or the tree beside the little cottage they had once rented.

Luke caught Abby's troubled expression and

shook his head. A look passed between them—for they both knew the problems Luke's stern aunt might cause. But the moment was interrupted as Duncan patted Abby's back. "Let's collect our bags and rrready ourselves," he said. "With any luck, we'll arrive in time fer supper. I'm eagerrr to meet Maria, the cook who makes those delicious meals ye've talked about, Luke."

The Scotsman herded Sarah and Kini below deck. As they followed, Abby heard Luke growl, "But I'm bound to lose my appetite once we get there!"

Abby sighed deeply as she followed Luke down the hatch. He was always hungry, but Dagmar Gronen had a way of ruining one's appetite and happiness. A keen loneliness for Ma pierced Abby, and she dug in her dress pocket for one of Charlotte Kendall's neatly pressed handkerchiefs.

Dear God, I want to go home . . . but we can't.

Abby crushed the hankie in her fist.

Please have Pa send word for us to return soon. And help us get through the next couple of months.

She lifted the handkerchief to her face and breathed in the scent of her mother's lilac water.

But more important, God, please keep Ma alive.

8

Chapter Two

The half-moon shed a pale light on the dirt road as Abby, Luke, and Kini jostled in the back of a buckboard wagon trundling through Pueblo de San Jose. Sarah sat wedged on the front seat between Duncan and the driver, a kind man who had picked them up as they hiked from Alviso. But the trek had taken longer than expected, partly because Abby had had to stop and rest. Everyone knew she'd inherited her Ma's weak legs, but it irked Abby to be the reason they'd missed dinner at Luke's aunt's, especially when they were all so hungry.

Now as the ancient horse pulled the wagon loaded with dried cattle hides, Abby watched Duncan open the silver cover on his pocket watch and hold it up to the moon's light. He turned from his seat and eyed them. "Almost nine o'clock, lassies and laddies," he said cheerfully.

As if in answer, Kini's stomach growled loudly, and Luke quirked an eyebrow at him. "Should be there soon," he said. "Maria, my aunt's cook, makes a quesadilla that melts in your mouth."

Kini rubbed his belly. "I be very hungry, Luke, so I don't think a case of ideas will fix it."

Abby giggled and leaned across the pile of stiff leather they perched on. "Luke's talking about a tortilla with melted cheese on it—a quesadilla. It's made from a flat piece of bread you fry on a pan."

Kini's eyes brightened with understanding. "Ah, new food to try."

Abby nodded, then glanced around the dark and silent street. She recognized all the familiar buildings on Main Street: Farmers Market, the small schoolhouse, Anton's Apothecary, and next to it a new establishment with a sign she'd never seen before: Doctor Harry Warbutton.

"Luke," she gasped, "the town has a doctor now!"

"About time," Luke grunted as the wagon plodded slowly by.

Abby's mind raced. "What if we could talk Dr. Warbutton into moving to Oahu with us? Then we'd have a doctor on our side of the island!"

"Can't imagine why he'd want to," Luke said, laughing, as he reached over and tweaked Abby's upturned nose.

Abby watched the sign recede in the distance. "I could tell him," she said with a sigh, "that he's desperately needed. . . ."

"Abby," Luke warned, "be realistic. By the time

we get back to Hawaii, it'll have been two to three months. Your ma will either be well or . . ."

"But we could ask him!" Abby insisted.

Luke shook his head and sighed, then stared off across the open, moonlit field they now passed.

His sigh touched her. Ever since Ma had gotten sick, Luke had grown quieter than usual. It was almost as if Ma's sickness had reminded him of his own parents' deaths. . . . *Does that mean Luke thinks Ma is going to die?* Abby's hands grew sweaty at the thought. "I need you to believe, Luke," she whispered under her breath. *O God, thank You for Duncan. He's a man of faith.*

Not far out of town, the driver let Duncan and the children off at the lane that led to Dagmar Gronen's mansion. "Night all," he called as the wagon creaked past them.

Duncan carried the sleepy Sarah while Luke, Kini, and Abby shouldered the satchels and carpetbags.

The lane, a quarter of a mile long, was lined with oak trees. Moonlight dappled through the branches. A gentle breeze, soft and fragrant, made the spring leaves shimmer silver in its glow.

Soon the two-story mansion with wraparound porch came into view, and the trees gave way to the corral, bunkhouse, and barn on the right. A horse stood quietly near the watering trough, its head down until Luke whistled. The mare's nose came up quickly, revealing a white star on her forehead. She sniffed the air, snorted, and trotted over.

"Lightning!" Luke said joyfully as he leapt up on the split-rail fence and leaned over to pet her. She whinnied a greeting and tossed her mane, then nudged Luke's hand for another rub.

"She knows ye, lad," Duncan said.

"That's 'cause she's mine," Luke said quietly, and Abby heard the happiness in his voice. When she pulled herself up next to Luke on the fence to pet Lightning, he grinned at her. "At least *someone's* glad to see me."

"I'm sure yer aunt will be too, son." Duncan, still holding Sarah, bent to retrieve the satchel Abby had dropped. "She sent me to fetch ye, after all."

Abby and Luke climbed down and followed after Duncan and Kini. As they neared the house, Abby could see that it was dark and silent.

But the small bunkhouse was ablaze with light and music. "The workers are strumming guitars," Luke said, glancing over. "That's unusual for this hour."

Kini looked at Luke hopefully. "Maria the cook will be up too? I be trying some case of ideas soon?"

Abby grinned. "I'm sure they'll let us have a snack."

"Well, lad, let's wake yer aunt. She'll be tickled to see ye," Duncan said with enthusiasm.

In the moonlight, Abby saw Luke swallow. She could sense his nervousness, but he climbed the porch steps and rapped on the door. While he waited, he turned back to Abby. She smiled encour-

12

agingly at him, though her own nerves were taut
with worry. She knew how strict his aunt was.

A moment later the light of an oil lamp glowed
through the lace curtains at the front windows.
As the door cracked open, Luke called, "Howdy,
Maria—it's me, Luke."

Instantly the door was flung wide and Maria, her
long dark hair unbound and falling below her waist,
was outlined against the light. "*Sí, estas tu!* Luke, it's
you after all." The plump cook gave him a welcom-
ing hug. When she pulled back, she gazed fondly at
him. "Your aunt will be glad to see you."

"I am glad you *finally* made it home," came a
stern voice from behind Maria. Abby treaded lightly
up the porch steps and saw Dagmar Gronen in a
dark green wrap, her iron-gray hair falling in a
frizzy mass behind her shoulders. She did not smile
as she looked Luke over.

"Evening, Aunt Dagmar," Luke said quietly.

Before she could respond, Duncan came up the
steps and smiled cheerfully at her. "Luke's been
a good lad," he explained. "Ye've a rrright to be
proud o'him."

"Mr. MacIndou," Dagmar said, ignoring the
compliment, "it appears you have done the job
for which you were hired. But why are these other
children here?"

Duncan eased Sarah to his other arm and
retrieved a crumpled envelope from his shirt
pocket. "Thomas Kendall has written ye, ma'am,

asking fer yer help with his children. His wife has come down ill, and he was hoping ye'd take them in until he can send fer them."

Abby watched Duncan hand over the paper, then twirl his handlebar moustache. Her stomach clenched. The twirling was a nervous habit of Duncan's, no doubt prompted by the unnerving glare Dagmar Gronen was giving him. One of her dark eyebrows arched while she tore open the envelope and scanned the letter. *Surely she won't turn us down after we've come all this way?* Abby held her breath until Dagmar looked up.

"I suppose it is my Christian duty." She tapped one slippered toe on the hardwood floor. "Come in, then, children. Maria will fix you a snack before bed."

Abby exhaled with relief and glanced at Luke and Kini. They were smiling at Maria, who began herding them through the parlor and toward the kitchen. "*Niños,*" she could hear Maria say, "I can fry some tortillas."

Kini positively glowed with anticipation as he followed her.

But Abby trailed Duncan as he carried the now-sleeping Sarah up the stairs. Dagmar held an oil lamp high as she led him up the stairway toward the bedrooms. "Mr. MacIndou, it is providential that you have arrived today. My foreman left unexpectedly two days ago, and I need someone trustworthy to oversee the spring roundup on the ranch."

Duncan paused on a stair, and Abby behind him. "Roundup?"

"Yes," she answered calmly. "It is time to round up the cattle for branding, but the men in the bunkhouse lack direction and discipline without an overseer. They are Indian *vaqueros*—cowboys—but much like children, really, who cannot be trusted fully. I will pay you well for several weeks' work, but you must start tomorrow morning at dawn and travel throughout the hills to gather the herds. Are you interested?"

Duncan looked back at Abby briefly. His dark gray eye searched her face. She wanted to shake her head no but didn't dare with Mrs. Gronen watching.

"I suppose 'twould be all rrright, ma'am. The children have been safely delivered."

Mrs. Gronen gave a half smile. "Thank you, Mr. MacIndou. I shall make it worth your while."

Sarah turned her head on Duncan's shoulder and sighed, and Abby saw his face soften. "Abby," he said, "perhaps by the time I return, yer father will have sent word fer ye to come home. Then I could accompany ye, Sarah, and Kini on the voyage home."

Abby bit her lip and nodded. *Perhaps by then,* she thought, *we can convince Mrs. Gronen to let Luke move to Hawaii with us—permanently.* Her nervousness over this first meeting with Luke's aunt was diminishing by the minute.

Mrs. Gronen appeared to be calm and reasonable, and it wouldn't be long until Duncan returned. Perhaps things were going to turn out all right after all.

By eight o'clock the next morning the children met up in the kitchen.

"Where's Duncan?" Luke asked Abby. He was already seated at the big oak table with a fork in his hand and a cloth napkin tucked into his collar.

"He left at the crack of dawn with the *vaqueros*," she answered as she sat on his left.

"Maria's been cooking up a storm," Luke said. He smiled admiringly as Maria set a steaming plate of pancakes in front of him. After pouring a dark stream of syrup from a little clay pitcher, he dug into the feast. Soon Kini was following his lead.

Abby and Sarah sat waiting their turns as Maria flipped the pancakes with expertise. Then suddenly the kitchen's swinging door burst open. Mrs. Gronen, dressed in black silk with her hair in a tight gray bun, swooshed into the room with a commanding air. She stopped in front of Luke, her hands on hips and eyes narrowing. Abby swallowed hard at her serious expression. *What's Luke done?*

"Young man," she began in a low growl, "you have shamed me in the sight of this town. You and

your little heathen friend there"—she pointed a
menacing finger at Kini—"shall sleep in the barn
from now on." Mrs. Gronen's nostrils flared in
anger. "*I* am the one with the money and power in
this one-horse town. If you would have stayed put,
you would be in my good graces. But you did not.
So first thing this morning, muck out the barn! You
shall work for your food, since you did not see fit to
appreciate my kindness when I took you in as an
orphan. You ran away from me!"

Abby watched the unfolding drama with growing
horror. Mrs. Gronen had waited until Duncan left to
show her true self! A vein pulsed wildly in Dagmar's
strained neck, and Abby watched it beat angrily until
the woman turned and pointed at her. "And don't
think *you* will be living the easy life! You girls will
be working in the house, cleaning, dusting, polish-
ing, and ironing. When that is done, you will go to
market, collect eggs, sweep. I warned Thomas Kendall about those heathen islands, but did he listen to
me? No, because people are fools. Now your mother
might be dying, and I am forced to take you in."

Abby's mouth dropped open in shock as Mrs.
Gronen flew out of the room as quickly as she'd
come. Sarah pressed back in her chair and whim-
pered. When Abby held out her arms to her sister,
Sarah jumped into them. Abby pressed her cheek
against Sarah's silky hair.

Maria put down the spatula and shook her head in
dismay. "She grows angrier each day." Wiping her

hands on her floured apron, she continued. "It's this talk of gold! No good can come of it. . . . But gold fever is spreading, and her servants are leaving."

"What gold?" Luke asked.

"It's been discovered east of here. The rumors are running wild, and people are acting foolish. They leave good jobs for a dream. So, *Señora* Gronen, she is not happy. No, but she is glad to have you here to work." Maria shook her head again, then bent back over the blackened stove.

"If that's how she acts when she's unhappy," Sarah said somewhat tearfully, "I sure don't want to stay here when she gets mad."

Abby glanced at Luke. His lips were pursed into a thin line, and Kini's eyes were wide with fear. "Come on," Luke said to him, "let's get the barn cleaned." He yanked the napkin from his collar and stood. Pausing, he turned to Abby. "I told you I'd lose my appetite."

"Oh, Luke," she whispered. All the happy anticipation in his face had disappeared. Those green eyes brimmed with pure misery.

Just then Maria set a plate of hotcakes in front of her and Sarah. The steam rose in a delicious aroma and butter dripped from the sides, but they just stared at them dejectedly.

"When's Mama going to be better?" Sarah asked in a small voice.

Abby took a shaky breath. "Soon—I hope very soon."

Chapter Three

"These are the supplies we need," Maria said as she reviewed the list one last time.

They'd been at Mrs. Gronen's for two miserable days—days that had been filled with chores from morning till night. Abby longed to go back to her little one-room school instead of working, but that wasn't what bothered her the most. It was Mrs. Gronen peering over her shoulder, watching her like a cat watches a mousehole! *It makes me nervous 'cause she's looking for our mistakes . . . and Sarah usually gives her a reason to complain.* Abby thought about Sarah drying the dishes for Maria and that plate slipping out of her hands yesterday. When it had shattered, Mrs. Gronen burst through the swinging doors and stabbed a long finger at Sarah, announcing she'd have no dinner that night. But Abby had secreted two tortillas in her dress pocket and brought them to her forlorn sister.

Maria now handed Abby the list. "Luke will drive you into town in the cart."

Abby nodded. "I'll take Sarah with me," she said, folding the list in half and stuffing it in her pinafore pocket.

"No." Maria shook her head regretfully. "*Señora* Gronen said she must stay and polish the silver."

Abby felt anger rise up in her. "I can't leave her here with that, that . . . woman."

Maria's plump arm came around Abby's waist. "It's all right, *niña*. I will watch out for little Sarah. I'll keep her safe." She winked and gave Abby a squeeze.

Comforted by Maria's kindness, Abby picked up her calico bonnet from the coat hook by the back door and headed outside. Luke was already hitching Lightning into the cart harness. The day was clear and sunny. Luke gave Abby a hand up, then flicked the reins.

As soon as they were out on the open road, heading away from the mansion, a vast sense of relief surged through Abby. "Oh, Luke," she said for the first time since the scene at breakfast, "you were so right about your aunt!" For most of the past two days Luke and Abby had been kept apart and too busy to talk to each other.

He glanced over at her and grimaced. "Told ya! She's a piece of work. . . . I don't know how I'm gonna stay here when you and the kids leave. I just don't have a reason to."

Abby examined his profile: the straight nose, strong chin, his blond-streaked hair whipping back in the wind. He was one of the kindest people she knew. He didn't deserve this!

"We'll have to pray she lets you go," Abby said with conviction. "After all, God let the Israelite slaves escape Pharaoh. That was a miracle. He can do a miracle here, too."

Luke quirked an eyebrow at her. "My Aunt Dagmar's a handful," he quipped, "even for the Almighty!"

Abby was beginning to understand how he felt, so she smiled sympathetically. As Lightning snorted and pranced happily in the noonday sun, she admired the passing fields of mustard seed and orange poppies. Reaching down into the basket at her feet, she withdrew her journal and pencil. The beautiful day had put her in the mood to draw. As they drew near the town, Abby sketched a picture of Luke's profile. The pencil skimmed over the new page. When Luke turned to smile at her sketching, she knew he was as happy as she was to be free of Dagmar Gronen's clutches—even if only for an hour or so.

As they entered town, Abby looked longingly at the schoolhouse. The kids were out in the yard on lunch recess—many playing hopscotch, tag, and jumprope. She wanted to go see her old friends but decided they'd better get the chores done first.

A minute later Luke announced, "Farmers Market." He reined in Lightning, jumped down, and tied her to the hitching post.

Together they went in and laid out the list before the storeowner, Mr. Jenkins, who began pulling things from the shelves for them. Luke and Abby carried the bundles and sacks out. "Put it on Mrs. Gronen's charge," Abby said twenty minutes later when it was done.

Their boots echoed on the slats of the boardwalk in front of the store as they exited.

"Hey," Abby suggested, "let's go meet Dr. Warbutton."

Luke gave her a funny look but agreed. As they entered the doctor's cramped office, a bell over the door jangled and the smell of new leather and medicinal herbs greeted them. Though it was dim inside, Abby's eyes adjusted quickly as a man in a white coat closed the newspaper he was reading at his desk and came toward her.

"What can I do for you, young lady?" he asked.

"Dr. Warbutton?" Abby gazed up hopefully into the face of an older man, who peered down at her through wire-rimmed spectacles.

"That's me. Are you sick?"

"No, sir. But my ma is—she's in Hawaii, in a place where there are no doctors."

The doctor pulled on his chin whiskers as he digested the news. "I'm sorry to hear that, young lady. Too bad she's not here."

"Yes, but . . . but I was wondering," Abby said, groping for words, "would you be interested in relocating to Hawaii? There's a big need for doctors there!"

He looked down his long nose as his glasses slipped lower. "Why, I just got set up here three months ago! Don't intend to pull up stakes anytime soon. But if I did, I'd probably be heading to the goldfields like all the young fellas I've been reading about."

Abby's eyes brightened. "You like gold, doctor?"

"Who doesn't?" he asked with a grin.

"How much gold would it take to convince you to leave Pueblo de San Jose and set up a practice somewhere else?" she asked.

"Oh, I reckon several hundred dollars would make it worthwhile," he said, pulling on his lower lip. "Most people are panning lots more than that, though." He walked over to his paper and handed it to her. "You can read about it yourself."

Abby put out a tentative hand and took the newspaper.

"Thanks," Luke said to Dr. Warbutton. "Let's go, Abby." He herded her outside into the bright light. For a minute she stood stock still with her eyes closed.

"Did you hear him, Luke? He said he'd probably up and move for a few hundred dollars! I've got to find a way to make that money."

"Abby, I think he meant he'd only leave to go make a fortune in the goldfields. Besides, this gold rush is probably just foolishness, like Maria said."

He gave her a hand up into the cart and flicked the reins while she cast him a disdainful glance. "I heard him with my own ears, silly." She stuffed the rolled-up paper into the basket of apples at her feet.

Luke shook his head as they drove out of town. "You heard what you wanted to hear."

Boys! Abby thought as she tied on her bonnet. *They never understand anything!*

As they passed the schoolhouse on the out-skirts of town, Abby watched the children filing into the building. Lunch recess was over, and she'd missed her chance to visit friends. Dejected, she unrolled the newspaper to take her mind off it.

One look at the headline story and Abby's mouth dropped open. Her voice was a high-pitched squeal as she said, "Luke, gold really *has* been discovered at Sutter's Mill! Why, it says here that people are picking it up out of the American River by the bucketful!"

Luke glanced over at the headlines, then quickly reined in Lightning. As the cart drew to a halt along the roadside, he grabbed one side of the paper himself and began reading out loud.

"The discovery of gold by Mr. Marshall two months ago has caused an exodus from the cities to the newly discovered goldfields of California. People are leaving the plow in the field, the hotel unattended, the store closed until further notice.

Many are asking, 'Why labor for money when riches lie waiting to be picked up in the goldfields close to Sacramento?' "

When Luke looked at Abby, the light in his eyes was brighter than she'd seen it in a long time. "Abby, do you realize what this means?"

"That somebody's going to get rich?"

"No! It means *we* can get rich. We could find enough gold here to take back to your parents . . . don't you see? We could help them buy the ranch!"

Abby's thoughts took off. How well she knew that Boris Rassmassen wanted Uncle Samuel's land and that he was raising money to buy it. What if Rassmassen bought the land before Ma fully recovered? What if he forced them out while she was still sick?

"The ranch . . . you're right. But, even more important, I could get gold to hire Dr. Warbutton to come to Hawaii!"

Luke was caught up in the article again. After a minute, he looked up with a sober expression. "Abby, it says here that the goldfields are wild—there aren't stores or places to live. I want to go, but I'm not sure your parents want you and Sarah to leave civilization. . . . Maybe I should go alone. Or with Kini. That way you'd be safe."

Abby twirled a sun-streaked ringlet with one finger as Luke tugged on the reins and urged Lightning away from the grass she'd been cropping. The horse nickered and kicked up her heels. As they flew down the road, Abby's mind was racing way ahead of the cart.

The minute Abby walked in the kitchen door of the mansion, she knew something was wrong. The house was quiet, too quiet. "Maria," Abby called out as she and Luke carried baskets to the kitchen table. "Where is everyone?"

Maria came out of the pantry and wrung her hands when she saw Abby. "*Señora* Gronen, she left for dress shopping in town."

"What's wrong?" Abby asked, sensing Maria's turmoil.

"*Niña*, I'm sorry! *Señora* Gronen, she grew mad when little Sarah dropped the tray of silver. She . . ."

Abby didn't wait for the rest of the explanation. She flew out of the kitchen, through the parlor, and up the stairs as fast as her legs could carry her. As she hurried down the hall toward the tiny room she and Sarah shared, she could hear her sister crying.

When she raced into the room, Sarah looked up, her face tear streaked. As Abby sat down next to her on the bed, Sarah crumpled in her lap.

"Mrs. G-r-r-o, Groo-nen almost h-h-h-hit me. . . ." Sarah stuttered and gasped, her face slick with sweat. "She said next t-t-time I d-d-drop something, she'll switch me."

Abby cradled Sarah in her arms while fuming silently. *How dare that woman try to slap Sarah! Sarah's too little to carry those heavy silver trays. Our parents have never treated her like this. But how can I protect her every second of the day?*

In that instant Abby resolved that they must leave before Mrs. Gronen did anything worse to Sarah. After all, hadn't Pa told her to protect her sister?

"Come on, Sarah. We've got to find the boys—there are plans to make."

Mrs. Gronen hadn't returned yet from town when Maria called the children in from the barn for an early dinner. They each took a turn at the water pump in the yard, then filed into the warm, fragrant kitchen. Maria smiled and fluttered about with dishes of chipped beef, creamed corn, green beans, and fresh tomatoes. They ate their fill as Maria hovered.

Abby could tell the sweet cook was trying to make up for not protecting Sarah. Wanting to set her at ease, Abby said, "The food is delicious, Maria."

"*Gracias,* thank you, *niña.* Save room for dessert!"

Sarah glanced up hopefully. "What is it, Maria?"

"Molasses cookies, still warm from the oven."

Kini looked intrigued as Maria brought a wide platter piled high with treats. Taking several, he closed his eyes after the first bite, savoring it. "It be very good! Like sugarcane at home, when it be warm in the sun."

As soon as Abby, Sarah, and Luke bit into the cookies, they agreed.

"All we need now," Luke said, "is some cold milk. Have we got any, Maria?"

She laughed. "Only in the cow! *Señora* Gronen said you must milk the cows now, too. Another ranch hand left today for the goldfields." Maria brought over a pitcher of cool water and refilled their glasses. Pursing her lips, she went on. "I cannot imagine leaving your home to chase gold! That's wild land out there! Snakes and bears and hunger. Why, my cousin, who delivered firewood today, says there are dark rumors going around. The goldfields are no place for children."

Luke straightened in his chair. "What rumors?"

"Oh, stories of *niños* being stolen by bad men who sell them as slaves or force them to dig for gold. Can you imagine? Little boys being taken for slave labor! Boys just old enough to work." She gazed around the table at them, and one dark eyebrow arched. "Boys about Kini's age."

The room grew quiet but for the ticking of the regulator clock. Abby's and Luke's eyes met in a moment of concern. Goose bumps raced up her arms. But the moment was broken when Maria asked, "More cookies?"

"No," Luke said, "it's time to milk the cows and get to bed." Abby knew him so well that his bold gaze at her before he strode out the door said volumes. *Time to get to bed,* his eyes were saying, *so we can leave before anyone wakes tomorrow. Time to get away from Dagmar Gronen's clutches—time to find our riches in the goldfields!*

"But I'm not sleepy yet," Sarah complained.

"You will be," Abby snapped. "Go up to bed and I'll be there soon." She grabbed the empty water pitcher. "I'll refill this for you, Maria," she said as she hurried out the kitchen door after the boys.

Dusk was settling over the ranch. The sky had turned hazy pink, and the evening breeze began to cool off the land.

"Luke!" she hollered.

He and Kini stopped on their way to the barn and waited for her to catch up. "What is it, Abby?"

"Well," she said a bit breathless, "what do you think about those rumors Maria heard?"

Luke guffawed. "Don't worry! Nothing's gonna happen as long as we stick together."

Abby rubbed her arm with her free hand to ward off the chill. "I . . . I suppose you're right," she said, giving Kini a halfhearted smile.

"I be ready to leave this place," Kini admitted. "Luke's aunt has no *aloha,* no love. Soon I want to go home, to my *aloha* people. Maybe this gold help us go more quick." His round, bronzed face smiled up at her. "Maybe it can bring more *aloha* to your mother, too."

Abby leaned over and gave Kini's thin shoulders a squeeze. "Thanks." She headed back toward the water pump and house, then turned to shout before the boys disappeared into the barn, "Sweet dreams and *aloha!*"

In the failing light, Kini's white smile beamed across the yard.

Chapter Four

They were far from the Gronen mansion when
the first streaks of light grazed the eastern horizon.
Kini, especially, seemed thrilled to be gone, and,
with the exciting news of gold, everyone hurried
forward, full of hope. Abby and Sarah walked happily
beside the boys, although each was burdened with
baggage, some of which they had tied onto their
backs.

They'd taken six moth-eaten blankets they'd
found in the barn, along with a duffel bag filled
with items apparently left by past ranch hands: an
old pot, a broken bar of soap, a tattered towel and
rags, two tin cups, four spoons, and three dirty
pieces of tarpaulin. "That will keep the rain off,"
Luke had explained to Abby. He'd also taken six jars
of Maria's stew, apples, a bag of cornmeal from the
pantry and, most importantly, a heap of cookies in
a tin. An "I owe you" note Luke had penned rested
on the kitchen table. It promised to pay double for
the food as soon as he made his fortune in the

goldfields. Abby had left a note alongside it for Duncan in hopes that he would soon join them.

Abby watched the folded-up newspaper jiggle in Luke's back pocket as he walked ahead of her through the sleeping pueblo of San Jose. When they veered unexpectedly down a narrow dirt lane, Abby spoke up. "Where are we going, Luke?"

"I'm gonna stop by Jacob's and pick up Sparks." He sounded determined, and Abby's heart melted a bit. For the past six months, Abby knew Luke had missed Sparks, the Border collie he'd brought from Pennsylvania. Now that Luke was back in California, it was only natural he'd want her back. But would Jacob, his school friend, want to give Sparks up?

It wasn't long before they arrived at the modest ranch house of Jacob Worley's family. *That's odd,* Abby thought. *There's no fire going this morning for breakfast.* She'd been hoping Mrs. Worley would invite them in for a warm bite to eat. Luke climbed the porch steps, knocked on the door, and waited. After a minute he knocked harder.

"Hold on!" ordered a cranky muffled voice through the door. As it creaked open Abby recognized Grandfather Worley, a wizened old man who was in his seventies. "What d'ya need, young'un?" Then he rubbed his eyes and peered closely. "Oh, it's you, Luke! Good t'see ya back, son. Well, the family's not here no more, so you've waked me fer no good reason."

Luke stepped back. "I'm sorry, sir. I was looking for Jacob and my dog, Sparks. Do you know where they are?"

"Land o'mercy, you waked me up fer that? Jacob's gone with his family to hunt gold. They done got gold fever, them fools! Ain't nuthin' good gonna come of it, I tell ya!" He turned around and was about to shut the door when Luke put out a hand to stop him.

"Did they take my dog with them?"

"The dog?" The man glanced around the yard as if Sparks might materialize any moment. He scratched his gray chin whiskers. "Well, it seems to me they left the dog here on account of it being too hard to feed so many mouths on the road. They just left a day ago. The dog might still be around here somewheres. . . ."

With that he slammed the door shut, and Luke looked wildly about. "Sparks!" he yelled. "Sparks!"

Abby and Sarah began calling with him. But it was Kini who opened the door of the barn and was greeted by the ecstatic leaping collie.

Luke kneeled in the dirt as he came barreling toward him. Abby could almost see the dog grin as he leapt joyfully around Luke and splattered his cheeks with wet licks. When Luke fell back in the dirt and the dog laid on his chest and whined, everyone broke into laughter. Luke pulled Sparks into his arms and squeezed his eyes shut.

"This is a good beginning," Abby said enthusiastically. *Surely God is smiling on us,* she thought happily. *We found Sparks and there's gold waiting!*

Sparks laid on his back, four paws extended in the air.

"Ha! You remember, boy." Luke scratched his belly while his tail beat the dust.

Suddenly the front door creaked open again. Grandfather Worley came out on the porch. "Young'uns," he called. "Take these victuals to tide ya over," he said, holding out a dirty bandanna with some food tied in it. "By the looks of it, yer heading to them goldfields, too."

Luke bounded up the steps and took the kerchief. "Thank you, sir. We are at that."

Grandfather Worley showed his toothless gums for a second. "This here's fer the dog," he said, holding out a rock-hard biscuit. "Don't think the mice can even sink their teeth in it."

He gave Luke the dried biscuit. Luke tossed it to Sparks, who leapt into the air to catch it. Then, turning to the old man, Luke asked, "Has he been good for you?"

"Well," the old man drawled as he scratched his chin whiskers, "reckon he was. Jacob was pert near brokenhearted at having to leave him. Guess the dog had to be locked in the barn or he would've followed their wagon. But I can see he's glad to have ya back, son."

They said their good-byes and were off, Sparks's

plumed tail wagging merrily at being included. As they headed down the road that would lead by the adobe mission, Abby noticed that Luke's free hand returned again and again to pat Sparks's silky head.

An hour later, the little group of wanderers veered off the track to tackle whatever breakfast Grandfather Worley had blessed them with.

"Mmm," Luke hummed. "Corn bread."

"Do you think Duncan will catch up with us?" Abby asked.

"Wouldn't be surprised. He wouldn't let an opportunity like this pass him by," Luke said through a full mouth.

"I'm gonna git me a bunch of gold and make Ma a pretty necklace," Sarah said. "Then I'm gonna make me one, too."

Kini wiped his mouth with the back of his hand. "Why this gold being so important?"

Luke looked at him in surprise. "Why, Kini, don't you know gold is worth a lot of money? When you get some gold, you can buy yourself a fine pocket-knife like mine . . . or all the ribbon candy you want."

"More clothes?" Kini asked. Abby smiled as she thought of how cold California seemed to the Hawaiian boy.

"You could buy the warmest jacket ever," she answered with delight.

"Yep," Luke agreed. "Everything your heart could want. "

Abby suddenly thought of Ma, and she knew Luke was wrong. No amount of money could guarantee health. "But the most important things, the best gifts," she said quietly, "come from God."

"Your One True God?" Kini asked. He'd been listening to Abby and Duncan talk about Him on the sail over.

"Here, Kini," Luke interrupted. He handed Kini the water bag, and they all took turns. Then they were off again, heading toward a future of riches— if only they could get there before the gold was all gone!

Late that day they arrived at Alviso Landing, where they caught a small sailing ship that ferried them up the bay. They sailed past San Francisco to the port town of Benicia. There Captain Shorty Marquez accepted their few silver coins and gave them passage aboard the paddleboat *Daisy*.

It was late evening when many passengers squeezed onboard at the last minute, desperate to get to the goldfields. Traveling up the bay delta on the crowded ship was as much adventure as Abby had ever dreamed of. In the damp cold air, they settled down on the hard deck. Abby and Sarah snuggled together in the spring chill under dirty blankets, and Kini and Luke settled down back-to-back for warmth with Sparks in Luke's arms.

In spite of the chill, Abby was soon lulled to sleep by the steady churning of the paddle wheels.

In the gray light of morning, a crush of passengers rising and making their way to the necessary woke Abby. She tucked Sarah in and rose to move about.

Though fog lay over the land, a morning breeze was dispersing the mist. Abby, who stood at the railing in her blue wool coat, could make out some of the landscape as they paddled upriver. Rolling hills swept up from the riverbanks in lush green mounds, dotted with orange poppies that had not yet opened to the day. Luke and Kini were wide awake now, too, and they made their way over to her.

"Want a cookie?" Luke asked, holding out one of Maria's delicacies.

"Sure, thanks." Abby took a sweet, soft bite and smiled at the look of bliss on Kini's face as he munched away.

His mouth trailing crumbs, Luke commented, "After breakfast, I'll go talk to some of the men over there." He nodded toward a clump of men dressed in wide-brimmed hats, flannel shirts, and work boots. "They look like they've come to hunt gold, and we could use a few pointers on getting there."

Abby and Kini stood in quiet conversation as a couple of strangers drew alongside them at the railing. "Morning, little lady," said the taller of the two men.

When Abby glanced over, she felt a jolt of concern. Although the man's dirty face smiled at her, there was no warmth in the grin. His hair, which could have been blond, was so greasy and unwashed it appeared dark brown. He sported a moustache but no beard, and Abby could see he needed one badly. His chin was almost nonexistent, slanting down to his throat, which made his bobbing Adam's apple stand out. He reminded Abby of a tall, skinny turkey gobbler.

His partner, however, was just the opposite. Short and fat, he neither grinned nor spoke. His hair was pale, and his eyebrows were almost white. In spite of a tan, or dirt—Abby couldn't tell which—he reminded her of a slimy night crawler that lived in a cave.

"Morning," she said and turned back to the view. She hoped ignoring them would make them move away.

But the tall man didn't budge. He gazed at Kini, and Abby felt the man was sizing her friend up. "So," he said, "where are ya headin', little feller?"

Kini hesitated, glancing nervously at Abby. "We be going to the gold."

The tall man smiled slowly. "Well, ain't that a coincidence. We are too!" He moved closer to Kini. "And where might your parents be?"

Kini turned to Abby, his face flushed with confusion. She put a protective arm around him. "He's with us," she said firmly. "Part of the family."

The man gave her a shrewd stare, pursing his lips. "Family?" He sneered as he moved off. "He's a horse of a different color, if ya ask me."

Abby watched them until they were out of sight, blended into the crowd on the forward deck. "Kini," she said, clutching his shoulder, "stay close to me or Luke at all times, all right?"

Kini shivered in his lightweight jacket and turned his dark eyes to her. "I will," he promised.

Later that day, they passed Sutter's Fort. It was a well-known outpost for traders, but they didn't stop there for long because the boat was already full. As they chugged on, the kids watched the river waters grow murky where the Sacramento River collided with the American River.

Abby had seen a map of the area. As the *Daisy* paddled up the American River, Abby knew they were heading toward Sutter's Mill, where gold had first been discovered.

The paddle wheels now slowed as the *Daisy* approached the small river town of Folsom. Soon they would disembark and hike the rest of the way to the legendary goldfields. No one but she—with her weak legs—seemed concerned about the twenty-mile hike ahead of them.

An overriding faith in easy riches colored everyone's outlook. Most were jolly with the anticipation of wealth. *Especially Luke!* she thought. He'd been talking with some of the miners heading up-country, and he'd come back in a high-pitched fever about gold. Although Abby knew how much he hated the way Dagmar Gronen lorded her wealth over others, she wondered: Was he still wanting the money just to help her family—or was he also caught up in the rush for riches?

As Abby stood alone by the railing just before they reached Folsom, an old man spoke to her. "Well, little sis, we've ketched the gold fever fer sure. Ain't nothing gonna cure us but to load our pockets with yellow rocks!"

"Goodness," Abby said, looking around at the crowd, "do you think there's enough gold for this whole boatload?"

"Why, sure!" he chuckled. "And I'm gonna git my share. See them men over there?" He pointed to three dejected-looking gents who were chained together. "Them's my prisoners. I'm the jailer for

Pueblo de San Jose, and I'm not gonna let them keep me home and miss this opportunity. No, sirree, they're gonna be gold diggers fer me."

The gleeful jailer rubbed his hands together in anticipation. "Hee-hee," he chortled, "the gold weren't discovered till the United States bought Californy from Mexico, did you know? Now the gold is all ours!" With that pronouncement, he leaned over the rail and spat.

Captain Marquez joined them at the railing as the slow gray waters rolled past the winter-greened hills. "Captain, I didn't know California had been sold," Abby said.

"*Sí*, yes." The captain crossed his arms and gazed at the distant hills. "Gold was discovered in January, but news of it never reached anyone until after the sale took place in February. Now many are coming from the surrounding areas to hunt. But as ships spread the news, they'll come from around the world."

The handsome Californio sighed, then continued. "Already, I hear that ships arriving in San Francisco are losing entire crews. Men are jumping ship, just like the farmers are leaving plows in the fields. My *amigo*, my friend, has told me over twenty ships lie abandoned in the bay. Even their captains have left to hunt gold! I would not have believed it, but my friend is an honest man."

"What will happen to the ships?" Abby asked in shock. All the captains she knew treasured their vessels.

"The boats, they are rotting. My *amigo* tells me some have been hauled to shore and the planks are used to build stores and hotels."

Kini, Luke, and Sarah had just arrived and heard the last part of their conversation. "You mean they are taking boats apart?" Sarah asked, looking up into the captain's face.

"Yes, *niña*. We will see many more strange things before this is all over," the captain explained. "And the gold seekers will find their share of hardships, too. Cholera has broken out in the crowded conditions of San Francisco." His eyes darkened. "And I hear the graveyard is filling up almost as fast as my ship."

Abby's heart tripped at the news. What if Sarah was to catch cholera? Abby knew the disease had no known cure. It struck quickly, caused violent vomiting, and often ended in death. It was her job to keep Sarah safe, and she felt a sense of urgency now. Pa didn't think she could take care of Sarah—at least not as well as he could, or Mrs. Gronen's servants. But with all her heart, Abby longed to prove she could.

Within an hour they docked at Folsom, and Abby sighed with relief at leaving the overcrowded paddleboat. As they clambered down the gangplank and headed toward the settlement, Sparks barked wildly, then streaked across the crowded commons. He raced headlong into a meadow of blooming orange poppies, then rolled onto his back, paws kicking the sunset sky.

Chapter Five

"I wanna go back to Aunt Dagmar's!" Sarah hollered. She threw herself onto a patch of weeds and refused to go farther.

Abby watched wearily from twenty paces behind, too tired to argue with her sister for a change. Her legs were numb from the knee down, and she'd tripped more times than she could count. Plopping down on a granite boulder, she thought perhaps Aunt Dagmar's hadn't been so bad after all. Her sweaty hair stuck to her scalp, reminding her of the many miles they'd hiked since sunup. "There has to be an easier way to get rich," she muttered to herself. Not only had they slept in the dirt of Folsom last night, but the map hadn't shown it was all uphill from there!

Luke and Kini, who were yards ahead of them on the trail, turned to see what all the commotion was. "Come on, girls!" Luke yelled. But he could see they'd go no farther tonight. "Time to make camp, Kini, and it looks like Sarah picked the spot." He shouldered his heavy pack and made his way back to Abby.

"Sarah has the right idea," Abby told him. "I'm beginning to think it'd have been easier to stay put."

"Ah, that's just tiredness talking. Tomorrow we'll be on the banks of a river of gold. Then you'll be so glad you came."

Kini grinned and headed over to Sarah. "Come on, Little Britches." He bent down and yanked her up. "You no want to sit in road where horses leave horse apples that be stinking."

Sarah glanced around in distress, and Abby and Luke laughed for the first time in hours.

"All right, we'll head over there and sleep under that oak," Luke announced. "There's plenty of water, since we're by the river. We just need to build a fire and heat up the last jar of Maria's stew. Then tomorrow we reach out to take destiny in our hands!"

Abby gazed at him in amazement. She'd never seen him so motivated before. "Luke," she said with a sigh, "you've got it bad. Sure hope it's not a terminal case of gold fever."

"I've never been so sure of anything before, Abby." He held out a hand to pull her up from the boulder, then absently wiped a streak of dirt off her cheek. He took her satchel and blanket, and they headed back to the spot where he'd left his own. "We'll camp here for the night, and tomorrow our hike shouldn't be more than six hours or so."

Abby groaned. He couldn't understand how tired

her legs were. The cramped muscles behind her knees felt like fiddle strings that had been tuned too tightly. She followed Luke wearily as he led the way to the old oak in the meadow. Although many had passed by them today, some on mules and others in wagons or on foot, their party had moved more slowly. Abby had to take more breaks than most. As a result, they were now alone in the gully.

Luke and Kini collected wood to start a fire as Abby laid out her blanket on a carpet of grass and wildflowers. Off the dirt path, the air was sweet with the scent of lupine, black-eyed Susans, and sage. The spring weather was balmy, the sky dotted with cottony clouds and an occasional hawk soaring on the updrafts overhead.

Sarah threw herself down on the blanket, and Sparks nestled beside her. Abby joined them with a happy sigh and uncorked the water bag. She and Sarah drank their fill. If there was one thing they didn't have to worry about, it was running out of water. The ever-present sound of the American River rushing below them soothed her as she lay back and watched a hawk cut circles overhead. How thankful she was that tonight was the boys' turn to cook!

When Sarah crinkled her nose and began to sniff the air, Abby leaned up on one elbow. "What's wrong?"

"I think you laid the blanket on a smelly pile of horse apples. Something stinks!"

Abby sniffed the air. "I hate to tell you," she said, her cheeks blushing, "but I think it's us."

Sarah sighed. "Come on," she said as she stood up and reached out a hand to Abby, "we can take a bath with the fish!"

It was late afternoon the next day, and Abby took a mournful look around. *We're here, and I should be glad.* Sounds of a mining town springing up from the California wilderness echoed with each hammer blow of those constructing shelters and stores. *Coloma is blooming like the golden poppies on the hills,* she thought. *But I'm too tired to care.*

A hundred yards away, Abby heard the sounds of a husband-and-wife team hammering that most precious of commodities—lumber. Apparently they had torn apart their covered wagon and were using the planks to build a cabin. The rough tarps that had once covered the wagon hoops were stretched over the square building as a roof.

Encamped around Abby were dozens of tents and lean-to shelters, homes to the miners who returned after a lengthy day of panning for gold on the nearby river. It was only natural, she realized, that a town should be forming at the site of the gold discovery, for every hopeful miner began his search here.

"I smell pork and beans," Sarah said, jumping to her feet. "Abby, I'm hungry. When are we gonna eat?"

Abby looked up from her spot under a pine. She couldn't even think about getting up right now. She was tuckered out from a day of hiking. Her legs ached fiercely. And Luke had insisted on going down to the river before building a fire or fixing a campsite. "I can't do anything until I rest a bit, Sarah. You'll have to wait."

"I can't wait, Abby. I might die of starvation! You sure don't take care of me like Ma would." Sarah shook her head in disapproval. "Pa's gonna be mighty disappointed when I tell him." With that she wandered off toward the couple who were building their little home.

Their fire, Abby guessed, was responsible for the delicious smells of pork and beans. Glumly she hollered after Sarah, "Don't go too far!" But Sarah had a mind of her own, and Abby's legs refused to keep up.

Abby watched the couple with something akin to envy. The woman, dark-haired and pretty, reminded her of Ma. And the man, though smaller than Thomas Kendall, smiled often, like Pa. She could hear them laughing as they worked. They had food for dinner and shelter for the night. Even their horses, which were staked nearby in the meadow, looked content.

Abby and Sarah would sleep in their dirty blankets

on the ground again. And, worse, Abby had discovered last night there were a lot of crawly things in the meadow grass. Once she'd awakened to the feel of a spider crawling across her cheek, and it had taken her two hours to fall back to sleep. Abby shuddered at the awful memory and glanced at the ground around her. But soon her eyes closed as she leaned against the rough bark trunk, and she drifted off to sleep.

"Where's Sarah?" Luke's voice penetrated Abby's groggy mind. She opened her eyes.

"Isn't she here?"

Kini kneeled beside Abby, his eyes full of concern. "Where be Little Britches?" he asked, and the worry in his voice woke Abby fully. She glanced around. The sun was setting and dusk was falling. Where *was* her sister?

She jumped up and grimaced at the pain in her legs. "Sarah!" she called in a panic.

Just then she spied Sarah's blonde head bobbing toward her, with a grin splashed across her face. "Here I am, Abby!" Sarah waved joyfully. Accompanying her was the slender woman Abby had seen earlier.

Sarah came toward them, talking a mile a minute. "This here's Molly. She's a real good cook, and she brought us dinner!"

Sure enough, Molly was carrying a fragrant pot in a dish towel. Her long dark hair was tied back in a ponytail, showing off her heart-shaped face and kindly smile.

"Sarah told me you've just arrived," Molly said. "Welcome to Coloma. I thought my husband, John, and I would be neighborly and bring you dinner." She looked around at their scattered baggage and asked, "Where should I put this?"

Luke cleared his throat. "We, ah, haven't set up camp yet. You can just set it anywhere. And thank you!"

Kini sniffed the air, his brown eyes glowing at the prospect of trying new food. "*Mahalo!*"

"That means 'thanks' in Hawaiian," Sarah explained with an air of authority as she introduced Molly Sampson to everyone.

Molly's friendliness quickly put everyone at ease. "Why don't you set up camp, then come join us for supper?" she encouraged. "We have plenty of food and dishes, and you won't have to worry about anything except eating your fill. That way you can save this meal for breakfast."

Abby grinned at her hospitality. "Thank you. We'd love that." The scent of hot beans wafted up to her, causing her mouth to water. "Where are you from?"

"We arrived a week ago from San Francisco. You know, the city has all but emptied, so we figured, why not? We brought most of the supplies from our store with us, and we're planning on opening one here for the miners."

"Is that what you're building?" Luke asked.

"Yes, it should be done soon. If you're looking for work, Luke, John could still use some help."

"I'll think on it," Luke said. Abby got the distinct impression Luke didn't want to waste time on that when gold was so close at hand.

Molly must have, too. "You know, we're extending credit to the miners so they can collect tools and get to work. Then when they get gold, they come pay us. You could do that, too, Luke."

"Really?" He looked amazed and thankful all at once. "That's . . . that's real neighborly of you."

"Well then, we'll see you at our fire in a few minutes," Molly said. "I'll leave this here for your breakfast," she said, setting the dish down on a tree stump. As Abby watched Molly walk away, she realized her first impression had been right. Molly was a lot like sweet, generous Ma. An empty ache churned in Abby's stomach, and it wasn't just because she was hungry. Molly's kindness had been too similar to Ma's, making her eyes fill with tears. Abby quickly turned away so no one would see.

"Sarah, good job in getting us invited to dinner!" Luke said enthusiastically. "Didn't I tell you, Abby, that everything's going to turn out great?" Though Abby never answered, he set about unrolling the tarps.

Soon everyone had arranged their belongings under the tree limbs. Abby and Luke tried to tie the pieces of tarp overhead to several branches, but the makeshift tent sagged sadly. "Tomorrow I'll figure out something, Abby," Luke promised. "We'll get some branches and build a lean-to like some of the others have. Before you know it, we'll have all the comforts of home."

Abby tried to smile at Luke's happiness. He didn't seem to have a care in the world. But she couldn't wait to go home to Hawaii and her parents' love, to a snug little house and a pantry stocked with food. To a mother as kind as Molly.

"Dear God," Abby whispered, "let Ma be there when we return. And help us find gold, lots of it, to get Ma the doctor she needs."

Chapter Six

"Luke? You leaving so early?" Abby's eyes had barely opened in the first gray light of dawn, but she could tell he was on his way out of camp.

"Don't nag, Abby. I'm just going to collect a little gold before breakfast. You go back to sleep. I'll be back later this afternoon." He was loaded down with the mining gear, a pickax and a washing pan, that John and Molly Sampson had given him the night before. They'd bent over backward, Abby thought, to help him. Of course, they'd also given Abby four plates, a frying pan, some beans, and cornmeal. As soon as Luke brought in some gold, everything would be paid for.

She sat up and rubbed her eyes. Luke was walking away through the meadow toward the river, Sparks bounding happily at his heels. "Land o' mercy, you have it bad, Luke." Had he even eaten before he left?

Now that Abby was wide awake, she smelled the delicious scents of coffee brewing and bacon frying.

She got up quietly, since Sarah and Kini were still asleep, and stretched. *Well, Lord, we're here. Please help us make this a success. Amen.*

With no one else to talk to, Abby soon noticed Molly and her husband sitting around their camp-fire sipping coffee. When they noticed Abby was up, they motioned for her to join them. Abby grabbed her journal and hiked the short distance across the meadow to join them. Their fire glowed cheerfully in the brisk morning air.

"Have a cup of coffee, Abby?" John asked as he rose to refill his own cup.

"Thank you." Taking the steaming cup, she wrapped her cold fingers around it and sat on a log next to Molly. The sun was just rising, the scent of bacon sweet in the air as it sizzled in the pan.

"My hair's in a rat's nest, I need a bath, and I sure would love a bed to sleep in, but at least this place has a great view," Abby said.

Molly smiled at her. "Camping grows on you. Sarah says this is her second adventure. Her first was sailing to Hawaii, but then you and Luke did all the 'best stuff.' Finally she gets to come here and hunt gold!"

"That sounds like my spunky sister," Abby said.

"How come you kids are out here alone?" Molly asked gently.

Abby took a deep breath and explained about her mother's illness and Aunt Dagmar's treatment of Luke, Kini, and Sarah. The couple listened quietly until Abby was done; then John spoke up as he removed the frying pan from the fire. "We'll pray for your mother, Abby. The good Lord will take care of her—and you kids—until you're reunited."

Abby couldn't speak for a minute. She looked down in her half-empty cup. "Thank you. You've been so kind," she said, glancing back up. "Can I help you in some way? Maybe pound a few nails today on your store?"

John smiled at her, and Abby felt his pleasure. "You don't have to ask me twice!" He flipped the flapjacks in the skillet and sat back down next to Molly on the log. She leaned into her husband as he put an arm around her. The two looked as happy as two peas in a pod.

"Would it be all right if I drew a picture of you?" Abby asked shyly. "For my journal?"

"Why sure," John said.

Abby opened to a new page and wet her pencil lead between her lips. She paused, taking in John's strong jaw, wide forehead, and short-cropped hair. Unlike most miners, John was clean shaven—"for Molly's sake," he'd explained the night before. Then she outlined their faces and began to fill in their features.

After a few minutes, John got up to tend to the fire. "Now, let's have some bacon and flapjacks." As soon as the words were out of his mouth, it seemed Sarah and Kini had heard, because they sighted the two heading across the meadow to join them. Molly just laughed and got out more plates.

"Next time," Abby said, "you come to our camp for dinner."

The day was full of work but also beauty. Spring was in full bloom; golden poppies and blue lupine waved on a gentle breeze. Happy sounds of men leaving for the river filled Abby's ears early in the day. Then she, Sarah, and Kini set to work organizing their own little campsite.

Afterward, they all joined Molly and John to work on their store. Kini and Abby pounded nails where John directed; Sarah delivered water and snacks to the workers and kept up a running conversation that made Molly and John laugh.

Now the sun was setting, and the balmy day was ending with a bit of a cold snap, Abby realized. She squatted near the campfire and stirred the pot of beans as she watched dozens of men return from the river, some carrying pickaxes over their shoulders and some just carrying a simple wash pan. Some came toward their tents with grins on their faces, while others looked dejected and tired. Some talked cheerfully and others were quiet. But where was Luke? He'd promised to return many hours ago, and it wasn't like him to break his word.

The sky flooded with thick gray clouds as the sun dipped below the western mountain, casting the land into dark shadows. A cool wind picked up. The tarps hanging from the pine tree now flapped like laundry on a line. *They sound just like sails luffing in the wind,* she thought. Kini returned from the river then with Sarah at his heels. He'd carted a bucket of water with him for drinking and washing.

"Is supper ready, Abby?" Sarah stood with her hands on her hips.

"If you'd help, it'd be ready a lot sooner," Abby urged.

"Pa said *you're* supposed to take care of *me.*"

Kini's eyebrows arched in surprise while Abby's eyebrows narrowed in anger. "If you want to eat, Sarah Charity Kendall, then you'll pull your own weight. I'm not your servant!" Abby turned away from Kini's gaze and heard Sarah stamp her foot angrily.

But Kini's soft voice encouraged Sarah to help. Several seconds later, Abby could hear the sound of plates and silverware.

When Abby's mind didn't calm down, she realized it wasn't just Sarah getting on her nerves. She was worried about Luke because darkness was closing in. How could he traipse off and not return before dark? *Now I have to worry about him, too!* she thought as she dished out the beans and joined Kini and Sarah on the dirty blanket. But she couldn't bring herself to eat.

The night sky grew darker with each passing minute. Sometimes the clouds would break and stars would show through. Abby took a bite of cooling beans. Still Luke did not return.

Abby began to think something had gone wrong. The river was dangerously high from winter rains, and more than one miner had been swept downstream. On top of that, she'd over-heard two miners talking today about a man who "got bit by a rattlesnake." He'd died, and no one knew where his kin lived. They'd buried him in an unmarked grave. He would simply never come home, and his loved ones would always wonder. The beans sat in her stomach like stones. *What if Luke's gotten hurt or fallen in the rushing river? What if he never comes back?*

In the distance, Abby could hear the muted sound of the pulsing water. Closer, the sounds of men around campfires rose to her ears. Someone began playing a harmonica, and the kids sat around their campfire listening.

An hour later, Abby saw Luke jogging toward them, and she jumped up. "You're back!"

The fire had burned low, but there was still enough light to see the grin spreading across his face and the sparkle in his eyes. "We're rich, Abby!"

He opened his hand to reveal four nuggets of gold shining in the firelight.

"Luke!" Abby picked up a nugget, warm from his hand. "How wonderful!"

Sarah and Kini jumped up and examined the other nuggets gleefully. When the harmonica-playing miner across the meadow began "Turkey in the Straw," the kids were spurred into an impromptu dance. Laughter rang out under the cloudy night sky for a while until they all sat down on the logs by the fire.

"We're gonna be rich, no doubt about it!" Luke gushed, his enthusiasm burning like a fever. "And here's the best part. I met an old miner—he's got a face like a shriveled apple." Luke laughed. "He goes by the name of 'Coyote'—in fact he kind of looks like one, with his bushy beard and eyebrows and a wiry little body—but he wants to partner up with me. Says he's impressed I made it this far on my own."

Abby drew in a sharp breath. "On your own? I thought we were in this together."

Luke sobered. "Oh, well, sure. . . . Anyway, his partner just died and left his tent empty. So you girls," he said, grinning at Sarah, "can have your own tent! Kini and I can sleep in Coyote's tent with him."

"What happened to his partner?" Abby asked, sensing she wasn't going to like the answer.

"Oh, he got bit by a rattler two days ago. But we gotta get back and take that tent or someone else will."

"Luke, we just settled in for the night. Can't we hike over in the light? I'd rather not step on any snakes or tarantulas in the dark." She'd gotten her first look at a black hairy tarantula the day before, and she didn't know if she'd ever get a good night's sleep again.

"Jehoshaphat, Abby! This is the chance of a lifetime. If you want to wait till morning, go ahead. But I have to get back tonight to claim the tent." With that Luke grabbed up a spoon and ate directly out of the bean pot for a couple of minutes. When he finished he wiped his mouth with the back of his hand and grabbed his gear. "Walk up the river a ways tomorrow morning right after sunup, and I'll meet you and direct you to your new home." He turned and hurried off without a backward glance.

"Did you see those big lumps of gold, Abby?" Sarah asked, her eyes full of pride. "Luke's gonna git rich, and he promised to buy me peppermints."

Abby grabbed her blanket and shook it. She wrapped it around her shoulders and sat against the tree trunk. "Go to sleep," she ordered harshly. "There's plenty to do tomorrow."

Kini and Sarah each wrapped up and lay down, one on each side of her, and soon fell asleep. Abby watched for tarantulas and snakes; the tarp above her blew wildly in the rising wind.

When the first fat drops of rain began to fall, causing the fire to sizzle and sputter, Abby

wondered if perhaps she should have gone with
Luke after all.

Sarah awakened two hours after falling asleep.
Thunder was booming overhead, and the sky lit up
with jagged slashes of lightning. A creek had sprung
up in the middle of their camp, and water coursed
across the ground as the downpour continued.
Their blankets and coats were soaking wet. Kini
and Sarah shivered beside Abby as all three leaned
against the tree trunk for shelter.

"I'mmmm c-c-cold, Abby," Sarah said again, her
teeth chattering uncontrollably.

Abby gripped her more tightly. "I'm sorry, Sissy.
I'm sorry, Kini." The rain splashed her face directly
now and again, so the tears of frustration on her
cheeks just blended in with all the water.

"I-I wanna g-g-go home," Sarah said, her voice
breaking and the sobs starting.

"We can't go home, Sarah. But tomorrow we'll
move to our tent." *If only I knew where it was, I'd
take you there now.*

Kini's thin body shook quietly, and Abby felt so
sorry for him. His thin jacket wasn't that warm, and
now it was drenched. He'd probably never been this
cold before, having lived in the temperate climate of
Hawaii. How Abby longed to be there now!

All the happy campfires that had burned hours before had been extinguished in the downpour. As Abby looked miserably around her, she felt as if they were all alone in the wilds of a strange and hostile land.

A twig snapped, and Abby's attention was riveted toward the sound. In the darkness she could make out the form of a man coming toward them.

"Abby!" someone called.

Luke!

"Over here!" she yelled back. Luke made his way toward them and grimaced when he saw the soaked blankets and Sarah's anguished face.

"Come on," he ordered. "Let's get you all to the tents. They aren't perfect, but at least you won't be out in the rain." He began gathering their belongings. Kini volunteered to carry the most so Luke could carry Sarah.

For twenty miserable minutes they hiked down to the river and northward along it, through the black night and pelting rain, then finally made it to the tents upriver. Kini and Luke joined Coyote in his tent, and Abby ducked low after Sarah and entered their own tent.

Here and there the saturated tent material dripped water, but it was heaven compared to where they'd been. She lit the oil lamp she found sitting on an onion crate next to a wooden box of matches and rejoiced to find a cot they could share. *No more sleeping on the ground,* she thought thankfully.

Abby found some old dry clothes the other miner had left, so she quickly got Sarah and herself into them. Soon they were dry and toasty, snuggled under warm blankets. The wind blew and the river roared close by, but she and Sarah quickly grew drowsy.

As sleep was just about to claim her, Abby thought of Luke: how sweet he was to get drenched himself to rescue them from the storm. Not only that, he'd discovered gold! *Soon we'll be rich enough to buy a home for Ma . . . and convince Dr. War-button to move to Hawaii. Good ol' Luke,* she thought with a contented sigh. *He always comes through for us.*

Chapter Seven

Abby woke, clinging to the edge of the wobbly cot. Sunlight streamed through the cloth walls, and so did the sound of the rushing river. Above it, Abby could hear Sarah breathing heavily, as if she had come down with a cold.

Pulling on her boots, and still dressed in the old miner's tattered pants and shirt, Abby gathered their wet garments in her arms and left the tent.

The sun shone so brightly that the wet tents steamed in the morning light. Raindrops glistened on bushes and leaves, and the ground squished with mud. Abby surveyed the area. They were camped on a little knoll above the flooded river. She could see Luke and Kini on the shore bent over, working. Several other tents and lean-tos dotted the area among the oaks, pine trees, and spring grasses, but the only other people she saw were men working along the riverbanks farther upstream.

A campfire the boys had built glowed with a crackling fire. Diluted by rainwater, a pot of beans still smoldered in the coals. She leaned over and took a bite from the stirring spoon.

A brown wren landed on a nearby branch of a tree. "Hello, little bird," Abby called. It cocked its head, as if trying to understand her words. Abby hummed as she spread their wet clothes on nearby shrubs to dry. They had tents and a cot to sleep on, the morning had dawned clear and bright, and hope rose in her heart.

Kini glanced up from his spot on the riverbank where he was panning gold and waved at her. Luke was dipping his wash pan in the water and swirling the water in a circle, gazing intently into the bottom. Abby hurried down the twenty-five-foot slope to join them.

"You want to pan gold?" Luke asked, holding out the flat tin dish that looked like a pie pan.

"Sure!" Abby rolled up her sleeves and squatted, her ankle-high boots getting soaked again. She dipped the pan into the cold river water. Luke loosened some sand and pebbles from the riverbank with his new bowie knife. Kini scooped up a handful of sand and dumped it in the pan while Luke gave directions.

"Swirl the pan gently at an angle," he directed. "You want the lighter rocks and sand to wash out that lower side. Keep doing it, Abby. The more that washes out the side, the better. Then you'll find the heavier gold lying on the bottom."

Abby worked the pan in a circular motion, but it

wasn't as easy as it looked. The water kept going in a circle. It took skill to wash the gravel out. Abby's legs grew tired of squatting. Finally, a quarter of a cup of sand remained at the bottom.

Kini leaned over her shoulder and pointed. "There, Abby! See the gold?"

She searched but didn't see the tiny fleck of yellow until Kini stuck his finger in and removed it. "That's the gold?" she asked, feeling that it would take about two years to gather enough to fill a thimble.

"Yes!" Kini said enthusiastically. "We're rich!"

She laughed at their happy faces. "You boys could charm milk from a rattlesnake!"

"We've already had breakfast," Luke said with a grin. He dried his bowie knife on his pant leg and slid it back into its sheath on his belt. "I'm gonna head upstream to meet Coyote at our new spot. Expect me back at sunset with the gold!" But just as he turned to leave, he drew a leather pouch from his pocket. "Could you give this to John and Molly for me, Abby? It should pay for most of our gear."

Abby opened the leather pouch and poured out a small mound of gold dust in her palm. It shone in the early sun. "Hallelujah," she said with a grin. Carefully she poured it back into the pouch and retied the drawstring. A squirrel chattered at her from his post on a pine tree, his fluffy gray tail switching back and forth. In the distance she could see Luke's back as he hiked away from them. A red kerchief filled with corn bread was tied to his belt, and it bounced as he hiked along the river—his pickax over one shoulder, the pan in his right hand, and Sparks bounding at his heels.

It dawned on her that she'd sure seen a lot of Luke's back lately. They'd been best friends for the last three years, and during that time he'd always walked alongside her—not away from her. And he'd always watched over Sarah, too.

Oh Luke, she questioned, *is the gold becoming more dear to you than us?*

"Abby!" Sarah's voice carried over the river's roar.

Abby sighed. She and Kini had been sitting on shore rocks, panning for gold for half an hour, when Sarah emerged from the tent in Coyote's partner's too-big britches and shirt.

"I'm here, Sarah!" Abby stood up and waved.

"Help!" Sarah couldn't walk far since the clothes were falling off her.

"Coming!" Abby shouted. "Here, Kini," she said, handing him the pan, "make us rich." She started up the incline and met Sarah at the campfire. Her sister's white-blonde hair had dried crooked, and her pants only stayed up because she'd grabbed a handful of them and was hanging on. "Oh, my!" Abby said. "We need to get you a belt."

Kini, tired of panning also, joined them and began laughing at the spectacle. "You no longer be Little Britches. We call you Big Britches now."

Sarah's eyes watered. She wiped her running nose with a sleeve that hung past her hand. "I'm thick, Kini," she said, her stuffy nose garbling all her *S* sounds. "Don't make fun of me today."

"I be sorry, Sarah," Kini said sympathetically.

"You caught cold, didn't you?" Abby asked, a frown creasing her forehead. She put one river-cooled hand on Sarah's forehead. It was hot to the touch. "Oh, Sarah, we need to get you back to bed. I'll make you sassafras tea and some hot cornbread. How does that sound, honey?"

"Thum honey thoundth good," Sarah said.

She let Abby bundle her back into bed and put Christine, her rag doll, in her arms. "You rest, Sarah. I'll take care of you." Abby toyed with one of her ringlets. *Just like Pa said to . . .*

"Kini," she said coming out of the tent, "would you go back to Molly's and deliver Luke's gold? I need some sassafras tea for Sarah. Oh, and don't forget the honey. Since we'll be making a big payment, maybe she could send some brown sugar and lard, too."

Kini nodded and took the pouch. Then he headed through the meadow toward Coloma while Abby stirred the fire and put Coyote's teakettle on to boil.

By noon Kini had returned, and Abby was removing her frying pan from the fire pit. Golden corn bread filled the air with a delicious aroma, and Kini sat waiting with a plate. But first, Abby took in a steaming piece covered in brown honey to Sarah. She ate only half. "I can't tathe it, Abby." She laid back down and closed her eyes, Christine clutched in one arm.

While Abby and Kini munched their own lunch on the logs by the fire pit, Abby watched an Indian couple walking up the riverbank toward them. The woman had long dark braids and wore a faded calico dress and rebozo shawl. She clutched a baby in her arms. The man, dressed in work pants, leather chaps, and a cotton shirt, scanned the area with a hand shading his eyes, as if he were searching for something. When they drew near, Abby saw they wore moccasins on their feet.

"Hello," Abby greeted them cheerfully. She noticed the Indian woman was gazing intently at Kini, almost as if she knew him.

The woman gave her a half smile and pushed a long black braid off her shoulder. Then she looked longingly at Kini again. "We look for our *niño,* our son. Have you seen?" She drew close to Kini and touched his raven-black hair. "Yano looks like you," she said to Kini. "Have you seen my Yano here?"

Kini's eyes softened. "No, I not see him. I be sorry."

"Has he been gone long?" Abby asked.

"*Sí*, yes . . . my *niño* is gone four days now. He never go before." The woman's anguished voice cracked, and she bent her head into the blanket-wrapped baby on her shoulder. She held the baby tightly, burying her face in the child's neck.

The Indian man, who frowned at his wife's distress, spoke up. "Some men come near our place downriver—ten miles away. They watch us, but I not think much of it. Then my son is missing. We hear some white men take Indian children. Now we not find Yano."

Abby's heart thundered in her chest. She had heard the very same thing from Maria! "You suspect your son has been kidnapped?"

The Indian father nodded. "We have heard it is so. These are bad men, men who steal what is not theirs. My son is happy with us. He is only eight years. He would never leave us."

Abby looked at the sad-faced Indian woman. "We will keep our eyes open for your son, Yano," she promised, wishing she could do more for them. The man nodded quietly, his mouth grim.

"Will you keep looking upstream?" Abby asked.

The Indian mother spoke up. "We will go on after our baby gets better. She is sick and we go back to our hut now. Soon we return." With that, they both turned away and began to head downstream, the way they'd come.

"Wait!" Abby called out. "Please have some corn bread with us."

The couple stopped. Though the husband appeared stern with a hawklike nose, a grateful look softened his face. Abby had already jumped up and begun to cut two large pieces of warm bread. When they came forward, she handed him both pieces, and he gave one to his wife. As they sat down on the other log before the fire pit, Abby smiled and offered to take the child so the mother could eat.

The woman turned trusting eyes on Abby. "*Gracias,*" she said, handing over the sleeping baby. Abby could hear the little child wheezing with a bad cold.

"I am Sopi," the mother said. "My husband is Toonatah." Soon Abby and the Indians were talking about all the change that had been taking place since white men had flooded into the area for gold. "We not need the yellow rocks from river," she said, shaking her head in amazement. "We need food— cornmeal and sugar. Toonatah worked for a ranch ten miles away . . . but the owner-man, he left for gold hunting. Now Toonatah has no work. We stay in a hut we build four miles downriver."

Abby thought quickly of the six pounds of sugar Kini had just brought back. *And we have some corn-meal left, too. Perhaps I should share some.* But food was scarce, and there was no guarantee Luke would find more gold. Silently she prayed, *Should I, Father? Should I share what I have?*

Deep in her heart, Abby knew what God would do. "We have some sugar you can have," she volunteered. "Have you got anything to carry it in?"

Toonatah's eyes brightened as he unslung the pack from his back. He fished in the pack, then handed Abby a tightly woven basket with a lid. Nodding with a slight smile, he mumbled, "Thank you."

Abby went to the tent and filled the basket with sugar. She also took an old handkerchief from her satchel and filled it with several scoops of cornmeal. When she brought them out to the Indian couple, Toonatah took Abby's hand in his. "*Gracias,* thank you," he said solemnly.

Sopi removed a small bag hanging from her waist. When she pulled out a nugget, Abby gasped. "Gold!" she said breathlessly. Abby's eyes sought Sopi's. "This is worth much more than I gave you. I can't take it."

"*Sí,* you take. You give us what we need . . . you give us hope that good people are here."

Excitement raced through Abby. "You can get more food up there," she said, pointing toward Molly's Mercantile. "And I will pray," she said, distressed for them. "I can ask all the miners, too. I'll find out if anyone has seen Yano."

"Then we come back soon to hear what you know," Toonatah said.

As the Indian couple said good-bye, Sopi put

a hand on Kini's shoulder and peered into his eyes. "Watch out for bad men, *niño*."

As they walked back the way they'd come, Abby shuddered. Maria had warned her, but it was one thing to hear a rumor from the safety of Pueblo de San Jose. It was another thing entirely to meet the heartbroken parents of a stolen child! Abby glanced at Kini nervously. *What if those evil kidnappers are still near here? And still looking for children?* Even Sopi said Kini looked like her son— like an Indian. *And Kini's just the right age to be snatched*, Abby realized. *He could be in real danger! Thank goodness Luke and Coyote will be back tonight. I'm sick of worrying over everyone. I need my best friend's help.*

Just two hours later, Luke and Coyote hurried back into camp. "Abby! I've got great news!" Luke said, hardly pausing to introduce her to the ancient miner standing beside him.

Coyote had a face that was more lined than tree bark, Abby thought. When he gave her an almost toothless grin, the crinkles around his eyes and mouth turned to deep grooves. He was small and bushy, just like a coyote. "There's been a strike in dry diggin's just a four-hour hike from here."

Luke's face was flushed with excitement. "A

miner passed by today on his way back for supplies. He said he heard tell of it, and Coyote knows that area well. This could be the big one! The one that makes us rich for life, Abby. We're going to check it out right now."

Abby stared at Luke in disbelief, panic gripping her. "But Luke, you said there was plenty of gold right here!"

"Too many men are moving in now. We've got to press on to new spots, Abby. I'm sorry to leave you again, but you keep the tents and most of the gear here. We want to travel light, and Coyote says there are caves around there. I'm not sure how long I'll be gone . . . probably a couple of weeks. Then I'll be back for supplies."

Abby's mouth dropped open. "But Luke, Sarah's sick, and . . . and I'm not sure it's safe for us to be here alone. And there's bound to be enough gold here for what we need."

"Oh, don't worry, Abby. It's so crowded here that it's turned into civilization. And Molly and John will help you with anything you need. What's wrong with Sarah?"

Kini piped up, "She be thick with a cold."

Luke gave him a funny look. "Well, a cold is nothing to worry about," he said, pausing as he packed to pat Sparks's silky head. "We gotta get or someone else will beat us to it. See ya inside of a month," he said as he retrieved his blanket roll and extra clothes.

Abby grabbed his arm in a death grip. "After our treasure hunt on Lanai, haven't you learned anything?" she questioned in a tight voice.

"Don't you realize this one trip could make us rich for life?" he fired back.

The cold gleam in his eyes scared her. "Luke, I don't want to be rich. I only need enough money to help out my family!"

"Don't you get it? That's what I'm doing. As long as I get there first." He jerked his arm free of her hand. "The gold is what's important."

"And we're not?" Abby questioned, her voice high-pitched with anger. "You always said you hated the way your aunt loved money. But you're becoming just like her!"

Luke's eyes narrowed. "I'll NEVER be like her!" He slung his pack on his back and headed out.

Tears stung Abby's eyes as she said, "But, Luke, we're supposed to stick together!"

Whether he heard her or not, she didn't know, for he kept on hiking.

Meanwhile, Coyote had been busy packing a pan and some vittles into his sack. Now he stopped and held out a curled-up hand to Abby—a peace offering. "Here," he said. "Give this to the little girl to play with." Abby stood still, too shocked to move. When he grabbed her hand and laid something in it, her eyebrows arched in question. "What is it?"

"Them's the rattles off a six-foot snake," he said with a lopsided grin.

Abby dropped it quickly, her eyes staring as the snake's tail rolled across the dirt, making an ominous sound.

Coyote chortled. "He-he, it can't hurt ya none! It's the wrong end of the rattlesnake!"

Kini was enchanted. He picked up the rattles and shook them like a tambourine.

Abby watched Luke and Coyote hike off up the river with a sinking feeling in her stomach. *What's happened to Luke?* she thought angrily. Then she muttered aloud, "Gold fever—that's what. And he's not going to be cured till he's filled his pockets with those stupid yellow rocks. . . ."

Deep inside, though, she couldn't believe that Luke would do this to her. After all, this was Luke, her best friend, who'd teased her, joked with her, let her win relay races even though he was much faster.

How could a cold strange metal change the very nature of a person's heart?

Abby clenched her hands at her sides. *Is Luke even my best friend anymore?*

Chapter Eight

"Kini, bless you," Abby said with a sigh. He'd played checkers with Sarah for two hours while Abby had tidied up their campsite and put some salt pork on to fry. She was thankful Sarah had finally grown tired of shaking that rattlesnake tail; Abby found it unnerving!

Earlier in the day when Kini had returned with supplies from the store, Molly had sent a gift of dried apples to Abby. It had given her an inspiration—"I'll make an apple pie for Sarah, and that'll cure her!"

Now Abby drained off the sugar water they'd been soaking in and poured the plump slices into her piecrust. She'd had to use the metal spatula to flatten the pie dough, since there wasn't a rolling pin in sight. But she'd found a wide stone, barely large enough, on which to flatten the crust. She felt happy as she formed a lattice crust top and pinched the sides carefully together.

Then she set the pie in the little oven she'd built

after Luke and Coyote had disappeared. In the fire pit she'd piled rocks on three sides and covered some burning-hot coals with river stones. She took the piece of tin Kini had discovered in Coyote's tent and used it as a top for the stone oven.

Kini watched with interest, for he'd had one of her dried apple pies on Oahu. Within the hour they'd know if the makeshift oven worked or not.

Meanwhile, a stream of miners returning from a long day of panning gold began to pass by their spot on the river. Before long, four stood on the bank below their campsite discussing something. Abby saw them and waved a hello.

One of them came toward her. "Howdy, little sis," the miner said. He took the corncob pipe from his mouth and motioned to the fire. "Whatcha cooking? Me and the fellers smell something delicious."

"It's an apple pie," Abby said happily. "And it looks like my little oven might be working after all."

The miner came over and peered down low into the oven. "Mmm, yessirree, it does look good. I ain't had nuthing but beans and salt pork for three weeks now." He licked his lips at the tantalizing aroma. "I'll give you this here chunk of gold for a piece of that pie when it's done."

Abby gazed at the dirty hand opened before her. His fingernails were cracked and filthy, but there in the center of his palm was the biggest chunk of gold Abby had ever seen. In the late-afternoon sun it glinted and sparkled.

"Why, I'm sure one piece of pie isn't worth that much gold, mister," Abby said, but Kini, who stood behind her, pinched her hard on the shoulder to quiet her.

"Little sis, it sure is to me." The miner's hopeful eyes bored into her.

"Why, I'll be . . ." Abby stood dazed for a moment, but Kini just grinned and invited the miner to sit down on the log.

"Sit here," he said, motioning. "Abby, I get plates. Look, his friends be hungry, too." Sure enough, as Abby glanced up, the three other miners were heading toward them!

They each took a turn peering in the oven at the golden-brown apple pie. "Looks flaky," said one.

"Looks juicy," said another. The third just groaned a bit and breathed in the scent. Apparently thrilled with their good fortune to have found a pie baking on the banks of the wild American River, each one handed Abby gold.

Kini ran and got the leather pouch, then Abby poured the gold dust and nugget from the three men into it. But the last one deposited on Abby's outstretched palm was a gold nugget as big as a man's thumb!

Her eyes widened and then met Kini's. Together they smiled as she retied the bag. Kini ran the pouch back to her tent.

Twenty minutes later, more miners stopped on their way back to Coloma. By now, the first four were digging into their plates of steaming apple pie. Most kept their eyes on their plates and were content to stay silent, but one piped up, "That's the best apple pie west of the Mississippi! I'll be back tomorrow for more, little sis."

Several men stood watching. "Can you bake a pie for us, too?" asked one tall man. Before Abby could answer, he hurried on to convince her. "It'd sure be nice to have a taste of home."

"All right," she said, warming to the idea that was taking shape in her mind, "you bring your gold nuggets, and I'll bake you a pie." At those words six miners burst into whoops, but the original four stopped smiling.

"Be sure you make enough for us, too," said the first miner who'd offered her gold.

"I will, if I can get more dried apples," she answered.

"Well, I'll pay for biscuits and cornbread, too."

Abby grinned and put out her hand to shake. The miner licked the last bit of sticky pie from his lips, stuck his corncob pipe between them, then pumped her arm up and down. "Deal," he crowed happily.

Abby beamed with delight. "The Rich Diggin's Bakery is now in business!"

Within three days, word had spread to over fifty miners that a little gal by the name of Abby had opened up a bakery on the shore of the American River. One miner had taken such a liking to his piece of pie that he'd offered to build her a much bigger oven, providing she gave him a free piece of pie for a week. Abby realized she could triple her business with his help, so she gladly accepted.

The next day they worked together to fashion a much larger oven from river clay and stones. Abby busily hauled wood and bark to the fire pit beneath the stone oven each morning. The piece of tin now sat between the fire pit and the oven, so the heat transferred to the pies above. After the fire heated up for an hour, the oven above was ready for baking.

Another miner heard she needed a rolling pin for piecrusts and whittled her one from a tree branch. Kini found her an old board in town, and she cleaned it with sand and river water and now used it as a surface to roll out crusts. When Abby ran out of fruit, she sometimes baked rabbit-meat pies. Two miners worked out a deal with her; they shared what they hunted, and she shared what she cooked with them.

Kini stayed busy taking care of Sarah or carrying messages to Molly's Mercantile. John began making deliveries on horseback of flour, sugar, cornmeal, dried apples, lard, cinnamon, and anything else Abby needed. She'd already bought every pie plate the couple had brought with them. *I can afford to,* she thought pleasantly as she rolled out crust for six more pies that morning. *Luke's been gone over a week, and I've barely had time to miss him.*

Sarah had improved after four days of rest and was driving Abby crazy. Once she'd knocked over the flour sack and sent the precious powder into the dirt. The pies that day had a bit more grit to them, Abby remembered with a smile.

Sarah now sauntered up to the makeshift table where Abby was working. "I want to help."

"The pie dough isn't to play with."

"Ma always lets me make pinwheel tarts!" Sarah said, pouting.

"This isn't for fun, Sarah. The men want pies, not tarts. This is to make money so we can go home soon . . . home to Ma and Pa," Abby explained, secretly thankful she was making money to hire Dr. Warbutton.

Just then Sarah grabbed a handful of flour and tossed it in her sister's face. Abby's eyelashes, nose, and cinnamon curls were instantly dusted with it. "*Ka-chooo!*" When she sneezed, some of the powder knocked loose. Sarah shrieked with laughter as Abby sneaked a hand into the open bag.

Poof! Sarah's face and hair were suddenly powdered like George Washington's wig.

Pie production plummeted as the flour went flying. It looked like a freak snow flurry had hit the Coloma area. Shouts and giggles echoed more loudly than the river as the girls chased each other down to the water, then splashed one another.

In a few minutes, Abby lamented their escapade when she realized the flour and water was hardening into paste in her hair. "Sarah, we better take quick baths."

Sarah backed up the bank in a hurry. "Not me, Abby!"

Knowing she couldn't catch her sister, Abby tried another tactic. "All right. If you want the rats and snakes to come dine on your hair while you're sleeping tonight, it's fine with me."

Abby sat down and began unlacing her boots. With a sigh Sarah joined her. Soon both girls were knee-deep in the river, splashing each other and shrieking as the cold water drenched them.

Finally Abby sat on the sandy riverbank and began scrubbing the paste out of her hair. Sarah joined her for a minute. Dripping, they hurried to the upper end of the meadow, where the sun still streamed down on some granite rocks.

"Let's lay here," Sarah suggested, her cheeks rosy from the cold water. "It's warm and toasty."

Abby rested for a while, feeling the sun warm her, then rose to go back to work. As she was leaving, the familiar sound of Sarah's snake rattle jarred Abby. "Sarah, that thing makes my skin crawl! Stop it."

Sarah sat up, her hair still damp. Her little blonde brows drew into a straight line. "But Abby, I don't have it with me."

Abby turned quickly and saw a huge coiled snake on a rock just three feet behind Sarah. Its tail lifted in the sunlight and shook an evil warning.

Abby swallowed the fear that rose in her throat. "Don't move!"

For an instant, her heart seemed to stop and she thought she might faint. But the terror on Sarah's rigid face kept her on her feet.

She quickly searched the area for a stone, a tree branch—anything to knock the deadly snake away from Sarah. She saw nothing within easy reach. But from the upper meadow she spied Molly on her horse, heading with a load of supplies toward the river. Cautiously she raised her arm and called Molly's name as loudly as she dared.

As Molly turned the horse and cantered toward the girls, Abby put a finger to her lips. Upon seeing Abby's frozen stare, Molly leapt off her horse. In a flash she seemed to size up the situation and drew a shovel from the horse's pack.

When Molly took three steps toward the rattler, it uncoiled in a liquid movement, its head soaring upward and weaving back and forth. When its mouth opened ominously, its forked tongue glided past fangs and licked the air, scenting its prey. Suddenly its head flew forward in a strike toward Sarah's white-blonde hair!

Molly, with shovel raised over her head, lunged at that split second. Abby yanked Sarah's arm, and her sister vaulted into the air.

Just as Sarah soared off the rock, the shovel flew forward and hit the giant reptile in the neck, forcing it downward. The head was instantly severed when the shovel struck the rock with a tremendous clang.

Molly dropped the shovel and ran to Sarah, who was sprawled on the dirt. "Are you all right?" she asked desperately.

Sarah began to shake and Molly held her close, rocking her back and forth.

Relief flooded Abby. "Thank you, Molly. Oh, thank you!"

Molly held out her other arm, and Abby rushed into it. In a minute, Molly began to laugh. "Well, girls, tonight we'll fry up that low-lying varmint and enjoy some bush steak."

Sarah recovered quickly. Always curious, she went cautiously over to investigate, then screamed.

Abby and Molly ran to her, only to stand gaping with wondering eyes.

"Molly," Abby said breathlessly, "you've chipped open the boulder—"

"And we've struck gold!" Sarah gushed. "We're rich!"

Abby's eyes bugged out at the vein of gold showing where Molly's shovel had chipped the boulder. "If we can just live through the experience!"

Chapter Nine

Luke tossed off the shirt he'd tied around his head for shade. Here in the gully, no water ran, no winds blew. The sun beat down hot. His lips were cracked, and his mouth was as dry as dirt. Even Sparks, who was sleeping in the shade of a tumbleweed, knew enough to stay out of the sun.

"Coyote," Luke said, mopping his forehead with the sweaty shirt, "where's the water gourd?"

The old miner simply pointed up the hill. Luke sighed and hiked toward the lip of the cave. They'd been here two weeks. They'd hit a small vein of gold right away, and Luke was sure there was more under it.

Up yonder in the shady cave was his bedroll and a small bag of gold nuggets. He knew Coyote had his own small stash. Why the previous miner hadn't returned, Luke didn't know. Nor did he care.

Now as he climbed the last few paces to the cave entrance for a cup of cool water, he thought of all the good the gold would do—as soon as they found the big vein. . . . Abby's family could finally buy their own place on Oahu. *And if I stay here a bit longer,* Luke thought, *and dig a little deeper in this old dry gorge, I might just get enough to buy Abby, Sarah, Kini, and myself a whole new set of clothes. . . . I'd sure love a wide-brimmed hat, and I promised Sarah a trunk of peppermint candy.*

He drank deeply of the cold liquid and smiled to himself. It would feel good to be the one who could do for others. He'd finally deserve the affection they all gave him. Thinking of a hat made him think of Duncan MacIndou; he hoped the Scotsman had arrived in Coloma by now to keep watch over Abby and Sarah. Duncan was a great investigator and would have no trouble finding them, Luke knew. Truth be told, he was feeling just a bit guilty about leaving Abby, Sarah, and Kini behind. Especially since he'd left Abby in the middle of an argument. But how many times in life did a body get an opportunity to make a fortune in a month? Abby would just have to understand.

If only that strange miner—a Californio—hadn't come through two days ago, Luke thought. Although the man had stayed only a few minutes to talk, in that short time he'd said something uncommon: "I see loneliness in your eyes. . . ." *It's as if his dark brown eyes can see right inside me. . . .* Luke shook his head to clear it.

He took another sip of water and wondered why he even bothered to reflect on the miner. They'd never exchanged names or shared a meal. But he couldn't shake the uneasy feelings that the Californio's final words had stirred: "Stay loyal to the ones who love you. . . ."

What's that supposed to mean? He doesn't know a thing about me, Luke said to himself. *I've never been anything except loyal.*

But Abby's last words haunted him: "Luke, we've got to stick together."

All I know, Luke argued with himself, *is I had to get out of there . . . had to give it my all to get the gold. Maybe then I can find some security in this life.*

Old fears had risen up since Abby's mother had gotten ill. It reminded him too much of the time his own parents had died in the epidemic, and he was left alone. But he didn't like to think about it.

Ah, that Californio is an odd one, Luke reasoned. *Right down to that strip of white hair at his temple that stands out like a lightning bolt in a black sky.*

Luke dumped the gourd-cup into the bucket of water and headed from the mouth of the cave to the back, where his gold lay hidden in his bedroll. It was silly to check on it when he and Coyote were the only ones in the area, but for some reason it made Luke feel good to gaze at the mound of nuggets he'd hidden.

Heavy. Solid. Gold. *It's not much yet, but it will be soon!* Luke thought, rejoicing. *Then instead of being the orphan who needs a family, I'll be the one to provide for the family I love. Gold is surely the answer I've been looking for!*

When Luke heard footsteps at the mouth of the cave, he tossed the gold back into his blanket and rerolled it.

"Get my gun, boy!" Coyote was panting hard, having run up the hill to the cave mouth.

Luke jumped up and grabbed for the old rifle against the wall. He hurried to Coyote, who had stepped into the cave and motioned for Luke to be silent.

Unnerved, Luke leaned into Coyote's hairy ear. "What is it?"

The old man grunted softly. "Grizzly bear. Saw 'im two days ago and wondered if we was gonna have trouble. Now I know we is." He cocked the rifle in readiness.

Luke looked out on the bleached stones of the gully. Pines and granite surrounded them. Few miners had come this way yet, but as Luke stood stock-still, he heard a rock roll down above their cave and crash at the entrance, then tumble on down the hillside.

"Grizzly's above us. Maybe he won't bother us, but maybe he's ornery and plans to keep pesterin'," Coyote whispered. "Either way, I plan on stayin' put fer the afternoon. No sense riskin' my hide, especially since this ain't turned out to be a big strike yet."

With that, the old man settled himself on a boulder midway in the cave. If the bear came toward them, he'd have a clear shot since the outside light would frame the beast against the sun. Luke's heart sped up at the danger. Rattlesnakes could surprise you. Hunger and thirst, landslides, drownings, and sickness were daily hazards, too. But grizzlies were a miner's worst nightmare.

They weighed a thousand pounds and could outrun a man. Their claws were four inches long and could gut a man with a single swipe. But what scared men most was their determination to hunt a man down. They could go anywhere you went and would follow your scent for miles. And once they'd made up their minds to get you, they kept at it until . . .

Luke heard a snuffling sound near the mouth of the cave, and the hair on the back of his neck prickled.

But he had nothing to worry about. Coyote had a gun.

In the early-morning light, Coyote looked haggard. Neither he nor Luke had slept more than a wink or two. Now they sat before the campfire, sipping coffee but keeping their eyes open. When a blue jay squawked, Coyote almost jumped out of his skin. He reached for the rifle, spilling hot coffee on his pants.

"Fiddlesticks! I ain't stayin' here no more, Luke. I seen what grizzlies can do. They're mean as stirred-up hornets and a hundred times more vicious." He shouldered his rifle and stood up. "I been thinkin' this gold vein is almost played out, anyhow. You comin' with me back to the river?"

Luke's pulse pounded in his ears. He wanted to head back, wanted to wash in cool water and drink that clear cascading liquid to his heart's delight. He hated this dry, hot work. Most of all, he missed Abby, Sarah, and Kini. He even missed Duncan. But the gold was still here. He could feel it in his gut, and he couldn't walk away from it now. He was so close to reaching his goal.

Still, maybe he should move on. It wasn't safe to stay in bear country without a rifle.

He opened his mouth to answer, but the words caught in his throat. The lure of gold was too strong, and Coyote seemed to guess that.

"Well," Coyote said, "I'm prob'ly just an old fool . . . you stay. You got the dog. He'll warn ya if trouble's near. And you got good legs, son. You can run a sight faster than me."

But Coyote's eyes said more than his mouth. *It's foolish to stay,* his crinkled brown eyes seemed to say, but Luke turned away from his gaze. So the old man went into the cave to collect his belongings and head out before disaster struck.

A few minutes later loneliness swept over Luke as he watched Coyote, his companion and partner, head down the gully with his rifle over one shoulder.

Sparks whined as if he wanted to go, too. But Luke only stroked his head quietly for a minute. "Come on, boy. There's gold to dig."

Abby rose earlier than usual and pulled her journal out of her satchel. Dressing in her green calico dress, she tied her flour-sack apron over it and added a blue wool coat to her shoulders before heading out into the early morning.

For a few minutes she enjoyed nature as she brushed through her long curls, then plaited them into a thick braid down her back. Squirrels chattered as they raced up tree trunks chasing each other, pausing with tails switching to watch Abby work on her hair. Birds flitted among the tall grasses, searching for insects and seeds.

It was cool and the sun had not yet reached the campsite. Abby loved this time of day when she had a few minutes to herself. Like the sleeping Sarah and Kini, even the silky petals of the orange poppies were still closed.

Abby stirred the coals in the fire pit and added dry leaves, wood shavings, and sticks to the fire. She blew on it, as Luke had taught her years ago. *Luke,* she mused, *is the very reason I'm up so early. Why am I worried about him?*

It wasn't about his physical well-being, although she often heard stories of miners who'd died and been buried without even a marker. But Luke had a partner who would watch out for him. Abby remembered the Bible verse that taught a friend is a good thing. For if one falls down, the other can pick him up. Surely Luke's partner would do that for him.

Although she was glad he was working hard to find gold, things just didn't feel right. She'd never known him to let her down, yet that's just what she was feeling. . . .

Abby sat on the log by the fire and opened her journal. The big family Bible, too heavy to carry, had stayed in Hawaii with Ma and Pa. But she had hidden in her journal some of her favorite Scriptures, dozens of them in her own handwriting, and it was to these that she now turned for comfort and guidance. One seemed to leap off the page at her:

> *Do not store up for yourselves treasures on earth, where moth and rust destroy, and where thieves break in and steal. But store up for yourselves treasures in heaven, where moth and rust do not destroy, and where thieves do not break in and*

*steal. For where your treasure is, there your
heart will be also.*   Matthew 6:19-21

Abby thought of the sack of gold in her tent,
which was growing heavier each day. In fact, she
was making so much money that she was now stor-
ing all new nuggets in one of the old boots she'd
found in the tent.

She was getting rich, yet she was sure her business
had been God-inspired. Surely there was nothing
wrong with making money, only putting one's hope
in money. And that was exactly why she worried for
Luke. She sensed he was trusting in gold and the
power that treasure could bring him.

"If that's true, dear God," Abby whispered,
"then You will have to teach him it's not the way
to happiness."

A moment later Abby sensed someone behind
her. She turned and caught Kini's happy grin.
"Good morning, Kini."

"Morning, Abby," he said as he bent over to
retrieve the teakettle. "You be speaking to your
One True God?"

"Yes. Are you interested in hearing more about
Him, Kini?"

Kini nodded and his smile cheered Abby's heart.
When he returned from the river and the teakettle
was warming over the flames, Abby decided to
share a verse from her journal.

Opening at random, she read, "Two are better

than one, because they have a good return for their work: If one falls down, his friend can help him up. But pity the man who falls and has no one to help him up! Though one may be overpowered, two can defend themselves. A cord of three strands is not quickly broken."

Abby sat quietly for a minute, amazed that this was the very verse she'd been thinking of earlier.

Kini nodded in understanding. "This be a true saying. I be glad to have you and Sarah. We be three strands of rope together." He intertwined his fingers to show what he meant and sought Abby's eyes for confirmation.

Grinning at his quick understanding, she asked, "Kini, how would you like to learn to read?"

"I can teach him!" Sarah said. She stood outside the tent, dressed for the day with her hair tied back with a leather thong. "I have a book, Kini, and I am a very good reader."

"It's true, she is," Abby agreed. "Why don't you two begin while I start on pies?"

Sarah beamed at Kini and leaned toward him. Abby heard her whisper, "Soon as I teach you to read, you can sneak into Abby's diary and read her secrets with me!"

Abby's eyebrows rose. "I heard that!"

Chapter Ten

"Abby, look at my fairy castle," Sarah said, holding up a flat piece of wood for inspection. Small sticks, pinecones, flowers, and acorns were piled high into the shape of a fortress.

Abby pushed a stray lock of hair out of her face with a floured hand. "Lovely," she murmured, bending back to knead her bread dough. "How'd you make all those stones and flowers stick together?"

"I made my own paste!" Sarah gazed fondly at her creation. "I'm bringing it home to show Ma. . . ." Sarah had been talking about Ma more and more often. But at the moment Abby didn't think of her homesickness.

"Did you get into my flour to make that paste?" Abby asked, irritated.

Sarah looked up quickly and grinned. "Yep! It's not just *your* flour, you know! Besides, I'm tired of work. It's 'Sarah, do this' and 'Sarah, do that'! I want to go home." She gently laid down her creation and took off running like a deer toward the river, disappearing down the bank.

Abby sighed. More and more she daydreamed of sailing away to Hawaii. Once she got there, her mother could take care of Sarah for the rest of *her* life. She would never, ever, under any circumstances volunteer for that job again.

The late-afternoon sun slanted across the meadow and the nearby river. Everything it touched turned to burnished gold. So as Abby pushed another ringlet out of her face with one dough-encrusted hand, she had to admit Sarah was right. Speaking to herself, she murmured, "I want to go home, too."

"What'd you say, little lady?"

Abby jumped and turned in surprise. Two miners stood close behind her. The tall thin one grinned, and his filthy clothes and sweaty odor made Abby take a step back. He had dark greasy hair, a beaked nose, and jowls that hung down. The other one, with a bulging belly that flowed over his belt, looked unnaturally pale. Something about them seemed vaguely familiar.

Abby suppressed the desire to move away. "What can I do for you?" she asked, wiping her hands on her flour-covered apron. In the three weeks she'd camped here, she'd never felt uncomfortable before.

"Why, just a pinch of pie," said the fat one.

"I'm out of pies for the day," she said, hoping they'd leave and never return. "You can buy some corn bread if you have a mind to."

The tall man raised a whiskey jug to his lips. He took a long swig, and Abby watched his Adam's apple bob. Then he wiped his mouth with the back of his hand. "Sure," he said easily. "That'd be right neighborly."

Abby paused. "I'm not being neighborly," she said. "This is a business . . . the Rich Diggin's Bakery." She nodded at the crude sign she'd made and hung over the oven. Then she headed to her makeshift table and lifted the clean rag that covered her baked goods. She cut two large slices and turned back to the men. But they were right behind her, so close she could smell their whiskey breath.

She was just about to hand over the pieces when she paused. "You've got gold?"

"Of course," said the tall, menacing one.

"But that little bit o' bread ain't worth much," said the fat one.

"Gold first," Abby replied, looking the fat one in the eye. Dealing with miners had taught her to be direct.

The fat one peered at her with narrowed eyes, as if he were sizing her up. Abby's heart tripped faster, and she held her breath, waiting.

Finally, he pulled from his pocket a large leather bag. He licked his index finger and stuck it in. When he withdrew it, a minuscule amount of gold dust clung to it.

She held out her left hand, and he wiped the dust into it. She sighed and handed him the two large pieces of moist golden corn bread. "Most pay more than this."

The tall one gave her a black look, then searched the surrounding area to see if anyone else was about the place. "Little guttersnipe's puttin' on airs, Gordo. What do ya think we oughta do about it?"

Abby took a step backward. She was alone . . . and for the first time since dealing with miners, she didn't feel safe.

Gordo grinned stupidly. "Usually we teach 'em a lesson, Bernie," he said.

"Just what I was thinkin'." Bernie took a bite of bread and moved toward Abby.

Abby's heart began to pound in earnest. The two men filled their mouths and grinned at each other, crumbs leaking through their lips. "Keep to your-selves," Abby warned, trying to sound bold and courageous, while her mind tumbled with fear. She picked up a wooden spoon from the table as she took another step backward.

Glancing around, she searched for a way out. It was too early yet for the miners to be returning from panning, and the strangers blocked her path to the river.

But across the meadow Abby suddenly glimpsed a rider and horse coming toward her. It was John! He was loaded with supplies, and Kini was clinging behind him. Abby's arm shot up, and she waved the spoon enthusiastically. "Hello, John!"

Gordo and Bernie eyed the rider trotting toward

them. Abby saw Bernie's eyes squint with anger as he said to Gordo, "Come on. Let's git outta here."

Before John and Kini arrived, the two threatening men had hightailed it toward the river. Abby could see their heads in the distance, apparently heading toward Coloma.

Sarah came up the embankment and ran toward Kini as he slid off the back of the horse. "Kini!" she shouted in glee, her eagerness bringing a grin to his round face.

John slung down a bag of flour to Kini, then dismounted and came toward Abby. "Everything all right?" he asked, pushing his wide-brimmed hat back on his head.

Abby rubbed her arms to warm up from the chills she'd just experienced. "Yes," she said slowly. Best not to mention her scare, or John might make her move in with them. Then she'd have to leave her oven and business behind. No, she'd have to handle it alone.

If only Luke were here!

"Good," John said as he unloaded a few bundles and carried them to her table. "I rode Kini back on the horse with me because I heard some rumors yesterday about kidnappers in the area," he commented quietly to Abby. Then he cleared his throat, changing the subject. "So, how's business?"

"Booming. I think I might be making more money than the miners who're digging gold."

John leaned toward her and whispered, "Don't

let the cat out of the bag, Abby. But that's God's truth. We're making money hand over fist. It's all supply and demand. Course, I hear about really big strikes all the time, seeing as we're next to the fancy bank that just opened. But as soon as miners hear about one claim, they up and leave the one they're at to try a bigger one. One fellow took over a claim three men left, and he ended up making a fortune. . . ." John shook his head. "It's an interesting time, Abby. History in the making."

By now Kini and Sarah had joined them and stood listening as John continued. "Why, I sold some goods to a fella yesterday who was chasing his mule down a hill when he tripped on a boulder. He looked back at what tripped him, and guess what? It was a fourteen-pound rock of gold!"

John shook his head in wonder as he remounted and then leaned across the saddle horn. "Course you and Molly found your own gold boulder," John reminded her with a smile.

Abby remembered how hard it had been breaking open that huge boulder, even with John's help. Then they'd all piled the crumbled pieces into Molly's wagon and delivered them to the Coloma bank. She, Sarah, Kini, Molly, and John had split the gold evenly. Abby had even opened her own savings account.

"Now don't forget," John continued, "if you need us or any more supplies, we're just across the meadow and up the ridge." With that he pushed his hat back into place and cantered off toward the rushing water.

"Let's look for rocks!" Sarah said. When Abby saw how excited Kini and her sister were after hearing John's tale, she shook her head and let them go. Maybe they would find a twenty-pound boulder of gold. She watched them rush down to the river. Anything, it seemed, was possible in California.

It was only later, when she was putting away the supplies, that it suddenly came to her where she'd seen the ugly faces of those miners before: on the paddleboat *Daisy*—when the turkey-gobbler man had been sizing up Kini!

Chapter Eleven

Luke was in a frenzy. His arms ached from swinging the pickax, but nothing could stop him now.

The day after Coyote left, he'd found the biggest vein of gold in the "mother lode." A veritable stream of gold ran just under the diggings they'd begun. He'd only had to dig a little lower, and the miracle had happened to him!

He chopped into the stubborn rock, his ax ringing out harshly, his arms jarring. But the stones cracked and chipped. He bent down and retrieved the lustrous pieces, one the size of a teacup. Dirty and unpolished, it still shone like liquid sunlight in his hand. He gazed at it—mesmerized for a moment—then tossed it, too, onto the blanket.

The ax rang out again as he continued to work. His biggest concern now was how he would get all this heavy gold back to their camp by the American River once he'd unearthed it. The gold was all his since Coyote had forsaken him! He would work himself to death before he'd quit and leave these rich diggings to someone else. *Too bad for Coyote, but fear has a way of robbing a man,* he thought.

Maybe I'll have to hide the gold somewhere and come back with a wagon. . . . As soon as I get back to Coloma, I'll be able to buy horses, a carriage, and a rifle. The rifle is the most important thing, so I can protect my gold.

The sound of Sparks's growls penetrated Luke's busy mind. When he glanced over at him, he saw the hair on his hackles raised. He stood, teeth bared, facing the cave. Luke's gaze traveled up the slope even as his stomach tightened in fear.

There on all fours walked the biggest bear he'd ever seen. Grizzly. Dark brown fur tipped with silver highlights, it was huge—six feet tall—even on all fours! It pawed at the bucket of water that stood at the cave mouth, knocking it over. As if in a daze, Luke watched the water spill down the granite surface, darkening it. Then the grizzly stopped, turned, and lifted its nose, scenting the wind.

The bear saw him and quickly stood up on its two hind feet. It towered over ten feet tall, Luke realized.

"Sparks," he whispered, "easy, boy." He didn't want a fight. "Let the bear go! Leave it, boy."

Without a gun, there was no way to win.

But the bear heard Sparks's growls. Taking the challenge, it swayed on its back feet and pawed the air with its front feet, its dagger claws showing. Its mouth gaped open, revealing fanged teeth the size of bowie knives. Luke's stomach rose to meet his throat.

The grizzly threw itself down on all fours and began lumbering heavily and rapidly toward them. The power emanating from the beast held Luke spellbound for a split second; then he let go of the pickax and instinctively stepped backward in a desperate hurry to escape. But he tripped and fell over while Sparks stood beside him, barking furiously.

Luke scrambled to get up and away, dirt clods flying and tumbling as he used both hands. He could hear the bear bellowing angrily. Sparks, as puny as a baby kitten next to the savage bear, barked courageously.

Dust clouded Luke's eyes as he began to run, knowing all time that a man couldn't outrun a charging bear that size. "Come on, boy!" he yelled in a panic, not daring to look back.

He could hear the slope giving way under the gigantic beast as it hurtled forward, could even feel the earth shake, and his mind could only register one thought: *Run!*

Then another sound penetrated as Sparks's barking frenzy crescendoed, and the bear roared in fury. Fear ripped through Luke as he turned back in time to see the grizzly's savage claws swipe forward. Sparks leapt to the fight with his fangs bared.

"Noooo!" Luke's anguished voice echoed down

the gully. The grizzly's claws hit Sparks in the chest and blood gushed forth. He was knocked senseless to the ground. The bear roared back on two feet, swaying above him. Luke had never seen any living creature as tall, as frightening, as deadly.

"Nooo!" he screamed again, this time trying to distract the bear from Sparks.

Instantly the grizzly dropped to all fours and lumbered past Sparks and on toward him. Luke's legs turned to jelly as they churned in the loose gravel, barely gaining ground. In seconds he would meet those fangs and claws.

The ground shook as the bear lumbered toward him, so close now he could hear it breathing. *I'm dead!* Luke thought. *Dead!*

Suddenly a shot rang out. In the next instant a gigantic tremor seized the earth, shaking loose rocks and debris from the gully. Luke turned to see the grizzly—fallen just six feet behind him with a cloud of dust still wafting up. He could smell the bear's musty scent. But the beast lay dead.

Swiveling his gaze, he saw above him on the gully's ridge a lone man, just lowering his rifle from his shoulder. Luke's heart thundered in his chest, the blood pounded in his ears, and his vision momentarily swam. But there was no mistaking the shock of white hair at the temple of the Californio.

Luke fell to his knees as if his legs had disappeared. Tears welled up in his eyes as he looked past the gigantic mound of bear to Sparks. His world seemed to come crashing down around him. Sparks lay still as a stone.

It took Luke a minute before he pushed off the ground and stood on shaking legs. He moved cautiously around the stinking heap of bear until he came even with its head.

It lay on its side, its jaw wide open, eyes closed. Blood oozed from a single bullet hole in its sloped forehead. Luke stared in astonishment; to hit the bear's head from that distance would take a near miracle.

He glanced back to the cliff, but the Californio was gone.

Shaken, he pressed on to where he'd left his dog.

"Sparks." His knees buckled as he looked for signs of life. His eyes were closed. He didn't move or breathe. From a wicked gash in his chest flowed a pool of dark red, staining the dirt. Luke tore off his shirt and stuffed it against him to stop the flow. "Boy, I'm sorry," he said, sobbing.

Tears turned into tracks of mud on his dusty cheeks. "It's all my fault. I shouldn't have stayed!"

But he was dead.

Luke drew one knee against his chest, and his arms wrapped around it. "Oh, dear God," he whispered over and over. "He's all I have. . . .

Help me, God." Memories of Sparks flooded him: how he'd come west to California with him, stayed by his side after his parents' deaths, kept him sane. Luke rocked back and forth in agony.

A movement of rocks beside him drew his attention. The Californio bent down on one knee. His eyes penetrated Luke's soul as he spoke. "I'm sorry about your dog. . . . I can see you loved him. But do not despair. There is something far richer than gold. God is rich in His love for you." He put a warm hand on Luke's shoulder.

Luke gazed at him, stricken. "God? He doesn't want me. And I can't trust Him." He turned desperate green eyes to Sparks. "He's dead. Abby's ma is sick, and I could lose her, too. Don't you understand? I could lose everything again. I'm . . . I'm afraid to trust!" Luke bent his head as tears rolled down his cheeks.

The eyes of the Californio were tender. "Fear not, for He is with you. God will not abandon you. Hope in Him," the calm voice urged. Luke balled his fists and his nails dug into the flesh of his palms, even as knives of doubt and despair stabbed his soul.

Luke felt the Californio's hand leave his shoulder, heard the clunk of stones jostling as the Californio moved back a bit. Lost in his thoughts, Luke forgot all about him until he heard a voice speak so softly that he wasn't even sure he'd heard it.

"Hope in Him . . . Luke."

When he heard his name, Luke looked up sharply. He'd never mentioned his name to the Californio.

But the stranger had disappeared.

Luke jumped up, wiping his eyes. His gaze roamed the area. In the distance he saw the lone rider on his horse, halfway to the ridge top. A sense of awe stole over him, and goose bumps ran up his arms.

Taking a deep breath, Luke fell back to his knees. His mind reeled with the impact of all that had happened. But one thing he knew for sure: God had sent that man.

"Stay by me, Jesus. I need You."

Luke heard a bee buzz overhead. Pine boughs lifted gently in a soft breeze. The world was quiet now, so peaceful compared to the devastation of a few minutes ago. When Luke closed his eyes, he could still see the thousand-pound bear hurtling toward him.

"You, You must love me a lot to spare my life. . . ." Luke swallowed. "Thank You for sending that Californio with a rifle . . . and those words."

Out of the blue, Luke remembered other words . . . words Abby had read to him from her parents' Bible: *I will not leave you as orphans.*

"God," he whispered, "I've felt like an orphan a long time now. When Ma and Pa died, I didn't want to go on. I was scared to come west, but I didn't have a choice. I wanted to run away from You—from everything. But then Abby and her family loved me. I'm beginning to think maybe

You sent them. And if that's true, then it means You've been with me the whole time."

The wind blew Luke's hair across his brow. "I'm sorry for running away, God. I've been so scared that I was gonna lose another ma. I'm afraid of being left alone."

I AM WITH YOU ALWAYS. The voice was strong, sure, tender. It surrounded him like warm, familiar arms. The words had been almost audible, and Luke's eyes roamed the gully. Tree boughs sighed softly, the sun glared off granite, flies buzzed over the heap of bear. But no twigs snapped. There was no one around.

Yet for the first time in years, Luke no longer felt alone.

The sun slanted and began to dip behind the distant ridge. Soon darkness would fall. A blue jay landed a few feet from him, cocked its head, and squawked loudly as if to shake him awake. Luke rose and found his pickax.

He chose a shaded place beneath a nearby pine tree and began to dig. When the grave was done, Luke bent and touched Sparks's silky head. "Oh, boy, I love you. You stalled that bear long enough to help me out." His throat got so tight it felt like a yard of cotton was stuffed down it.

Swallowing, he continued. "You stayed by me, right to the end. . . . But now I have Someone who'll stay with me forever. And somehow, Sparks, I know it will be all right."

Luke gently carried him to the grave.

As he retrieved his belongings from the cave, all he could think about was heading back to Coloma. He dumped his small stash of gold into his knapsack and never looked back at the rich vein of the mother lode he'd come upon. It could stay in the ground for all he cared.

The sun sank completely behind the mountains. Luke knew exactly where he'd camp for the night; he'd passed a shallow branch of the river on the way here. Along its bank was a wooded glen with an old rowboat on the bank. He'd make a fire to keep away wild animals and sleep a little. At first light, he'd start back to Coloma—and to Abby. He missed her powerfully now.

Chapter Twelve

"Red sky at night, sailors' delight," Abby said, pausing at the water's edge as she cleaned off the board she used to roll out piecrusts. The river lapped at her feet as she studied the hazy, pink sky and tried to ignore the nervousness in her stomach.

True, Sarah and Kini should have been back before now. The walk to Molly's Mercantile only took twenty minutes. But they'd probably turned down Main Street to peer in some new shop windows and lost track of time.

Abby drained the water from the clean board and tucked it under her arm as she started back up the incline. She stood it on end against a tree trunk and gazed around the campsite. It was lonely without Sarah and Kini.

She paced for a few minutes, praying silently. As the sun began its descent behind the distant mountains, her nerves stetched taut. "Where are they?" she whispered to herself.

Now her worry escalated to anger. "When I find

you, Sarah Charity Kendall, you'll wish you had come home on time!"

Abby picked up her mixing bowl, crusted with dried corn bread batter, and headed down to the river again. Angrily, she scooped sand into the bowl and rubbed it against the insides. The batter loosened and mixed with the river water. Abby watched the white swirl of liquid speed away down the river.

Glancing at the sunset again, Abby saw an eagle swoop from a tall pine and soar above the river, which was now painted crimson by the light. When the graceful bird of prey dove toward the water's surface, its outstretched talons dragged the water and lifted a struggling trout. Droplets rained down as the fish fought against the grip and certain death, but to no avail. The eagle flapped its huge wings and rose up and away over the treetops, disappearing from view.

Abby groaned in dismay. What if Kini had also been snatched like a trout—by those kidnappers stealing Indian children? But if he had, then where was Sarah?

She hurried back to camp and fetched her coat. Lighting the lantern, Abby began her trek down the river and across the meadow to Molly's.

Twenty minutes later she reached the mercantile and didn't bother to knock. She walked right into the cheerful store with the small bedroom and kitchen at the back.

Molly gave her a happy greeting but sobered when Abby asked what time Sarah and Kini had left.

"Why, they never came here today," Molly assured her. Then, seeing the horror on Abby's face, she drew Abby close. They had spoken before about the Indian couple and the missing children. "Oh, honey, I'm so sorry."

"What if those kidnappers have taken Kini— and Sarah? Oh, Molly, what should I do?" Abby's face had grown pale.

"John's gone to Sacramento for supplies. As soon as he gets back tomorrow afternoon, he'll organize a search party."

Abby put a hand over her mouth. If Molly thought it was possible, her worst fear *had* come true! Stricken with terror, one thought dominated her mind. *Pa was right! He told me I couldn't take care of Sarah—and he's right!*

"You're going to stay here with me tonight," Molly admonished. "You can sleep right alongside me, and in the morning we'll both hunt through town and backtrack to your campsite."

A tremor ran through Abby. Sarah and Kini had been stolen—now she was sure of it. Would they be sold into slavery or forced to dig for gold? Who had taken them? And could she find them in time, before they were taken beyond her reach—like that poor trout snatched from his river home and carried on the dizzying heights?

Abby lay wide awake in Molly's bed. Every time she closed her eyes, she saw the ugly face of Bernie, the whiskey-swilling turkey gobbler . . . kidnapper! She was sure it had been him and his pale worm of a friend, Gordo, who had taken Kini and Sarah.

Dearest God, she prayed in desperation, *help me!*

The next moment she thought of Luke, and her heart burned in anger against him. *If you'd been here, where you belong, this wouldn't have happened!* But even so, she wished he were there with her. As irresponsible as he'd been lately, she knew Luke would do anything to help.

Despair swamped her as she turned on her side, tears sliding silently down her cheeks and wetting the pillow. *If anything happens to Sarah, it'll be the death of Ma!*

Abby's stomach was in a knot. During the two hours she'd slept, she'd had terrible nightmares. Quietly she slid from the bed and dressed by the light of the moon. She couldn't wait until John got back. He could organize a search party when he got home. She would begin the search now.

Abby scratched a note on a piece of brown wrapping paper, saying she was borrowing the horse, and left it on Molly's kitchen table. Then she slipped out the back door. She unhooked the bridle from the cabin wall and carried it to Sweet Pea, Molly's mare, who was staked in the meadow grass nearby. She led the horse to a nearby stump and buckled on her bridle. Then Abby threw on her blanket, climbed the stump, and mounted bareback.

She couldn't shake the horrible memory of the Indian couple whose son had been kidnapped. *If Kini's been taken for the same reason, where on earth should I start looking? He and Sarah could be anywhere!*

But even as she tugged the reins and gently pressed her legs into the mare's side, she knew instinctively where she had to go. Upriver. Anyone doing such an evil deed would head away from civilization. And that means into wilder territory, farther up the American River—into no-man's-land.

Luke had slept longer than he intended. The morning was well on its way when he opened his eyes. "Must've been pretty tired," he mused to himself. Now he rose and splashed water behind his ears and over his face. His heart still ached over losing Sparks. But somehow a new hope, a new freedom from fear, was growing in his chest.

He breakfasted on jerky and rock-hard biscuits, then headed south following the tributary that would merge with the south fork of the American River.

He'd been hiking awhile when he heard voices. Since he was inland from the main river, he decided not to check it out. He was eager to get back to Abby, Sarah, and Kini. But in the distance he saw smoke rising from someone's cook fire. Miners were everywhere now, but he thought it odd that the voices he'd heard were young and high-pitched, not like men's.

Twenty minutes later, Luke had made his way down to the American River for a drink when he spotted a rider in the distance. As he sat on a river rock, he watched the rider come closer.

It was a woman, or girl, with long tea-colored hair like Abby's. *Could it be?* he wondered. He pushed off the rock and began hiking quickly toward the rider.

Abby's heart sped up. Someone was walking on the river's shore toward her, and it looked like . . .

"Abby!" she heard Luke call.

Her eyes stung with tears as she dug in her heels, forcing Sweet Pea into a trot. Luke waited, a grin dimpling his cheek, until she got to him. Then he saw the look on her face.

"Abby, what's wrong?"

She slid one leg over Sweet Pea's neck, and Luke caught her. Her eyes brimmed with tears. "Sarah and Kini are missing."

Luke searched her face. "What do you mean—missing?"

"Some men took them, like they've been kidnapping Indian children—the way Maria told us. I think they were after Kini, but Sarah was with him. They took her, too!" She buried her face in her hands and wept. Gasping for air between sobs, she lamented, "Pa was right . . . I can't take care of Sarah! I'm a failure!"

Luke pulled her close and let her cry it out. "Shhh . . . that's not true." He held her off at arm's length and gazed at her. "Seems to me you nursed her through a cold, fed her every day, and kept her safe at camp."

But his words only started the tears again. "B-b-b-but I d-d-didn't!" she stuttered.

"Posh!" Luke scolded. "Not even your ma watches Sarah twenty-four hours a day, Abby. You couldn't help this." He put an arm around her and took the reins as he led her back the way he'd come. Sitting on a wide boulder, he said, "But I know Someone who can help us." Then he began to recount his own recent story of help and hope.

Ten minutes later, Abby jumped up from the log she'd been sitting on. She paced a minute, then turned back to Luke. "You almost got killed by a grizzly? How'd you escape?"

"A stranger shot the bear. In the dead center of his forehead at fifty paces!"

Abby's mouth dropped open. "Honest?"

"God's truth. He was a Californio with a streak of white hair at his temple. I'll never forget the look in his eyes when he said . . ." Luke stopped, as if it were hard to repeat the words. "'God is rich in His love for you.'"

"Abby,"—Luke's face was a mask of awe at the memory—"he said my name, but I never told him my name."

Abby's brilliant blue eyes glowed with an inner light. "I believe you," she said. "He was an answer to a prayer." Then she quieted, waiting for him to go on. He had told her about Sparks's death and the stranger's words, but now he shared his talk with God.

Luke stared at the ground, scuffing the dirt with the toe of one boot, then looked up again. "I was wrong about the gold. It wasn't the important thing at all. Can you forgive me for leaving all of you?"

Tears dribbled over Abby's eyelashes. "You old coon. You're my best friend. Of course I forgive you."

Luke grinned sheepishly, then swept her into a hug. "What a relief!" He twirled her in a circle and Abby's unkempt braid came completely undone, but she laughed.

"Now," Luke said with determination, "let's go find Sarah and Kini and bring them home."

He gave Abby a leg up on Sweet Pea, then mounted behind her and urged the mare back the way he'd come. Abby was right; the kidnappers would head away from civilization and into the wilds.

Abby sighed deeply as the horse's hoofs clacked against the river stones and carried them along the watercourse. *Luke is finally right with God!* In spite of her worry over Sarah and Kini, her heart soared with his good news.

"Maybe we should ask Jesus what to do," she suggested. "After all, He's watching Sarah and Kini right now."

"Good idea," Luke agreed. Then his voice rang out above the river's roar as he prayed for God's guidance and help.

Chapter Thirteen

Luke shared his jerky with Abby, and while they ate, he thought about where kidnappers might go. It made sense to travel along the riverbank, as Abby had been doing. The further up you went, the less picked over the gold was. Besides, he was pretty sure he'd have seen or heard something inland if a lot of kids were involved, for he'd come that way.

Then Luke remembered the voices he'd heard about an hour's walk back. The sounds had been coming from the river, and the voices had seemed too high-pitched for men.

"Abby, I think I know where they might be." Luke stashed the food back in his pack. "Aways back I heard voices, but they weren't men's voices. I didn't think much of it at the time, but I just realized it could be those kidnapped kids."

Abby jumped up, fire burning in her blue eyes. "Let's go!" Luke held Sweet Pea's bridle while Abby climbed on a log to mount up.

A couple of miles later, Luke reined in the mare. "We could come on them any time now. Since we don't want to give ourselves away, let's head inland and sneak up from behind." They intersected with his original trail. Not long afterward, Abby spotted smoke rising in the distance and pointed it out.

"Good eyesight," Luke said. He helped her down from Sweet Pea. "Let's leave the horse here while we check out the lay of the land."

Abby grinned. "You sound like a general leading his troops."

"Well, this could be a battle. Keep your head down! We need the element of surprise since we don't have a rifle."

They stole through the trees toward the distant river. After several minutes of hiking, Luke motioned for them to crouch behind a massive boulder. They could hear the river from there. Abby peered around the rock, and what she saw made her heart pick up speed.

A log cabin sat in a clearing. From its chimney, smoke issued forth. Beyond lay the river, rushing silver in the afternoon light. A man sat in a crude chair overlooking the water, a rifle stretched across his knees. His back was to them as he watched or guarded something.

Luke and Abby moved cautiously, sneaking from

tree to bush to boulder in a crouch. Soon they were close to the small cabin. As they passed, the opened door revealed a rustic room with a table and benches. It appeared no one was inside. Abby could see a fire burning low in the fireplace and a charred pot suspended above it. Even from a distance Abby could smell stew simmering.

Near the cabin, chains were wrapped around tree trunks. "So they chain up the children when they're not working!" Luke whispered. Anger boiled up in Abby at the thought of Sarah and Kini chained. The two pressed on toward the river to discover what that man was guarding.

Making a wide arc around him, Abby and Luke came near the shore and hid behind a stand of trees about twelve feet from the water. Their eyes roamed the river, and Abby found what they'd been searching for.

She counted three, four, five children standing in different spots along the bank, each one bent over and panning under the watchful gaze of . . . "Bernie!" Abby barely breathed the words. She could now clearly make out his chinless face and dark stringy hair. Beside him sat a jug of liquor, which he guzzled from. Down the bank another man sat in the shade.

"Who's that?" Luke asked, nodding toward the distant man.

"Gordo," she answered, almost spitting out his name.

Their eyes swept back to the children, all of them dark-haired Indians, but each of different age and build. As they searched for Kini among them, Abby spied him first. "Kini!" she whispered, instinctively heading toward him.

"No!" Luke grabbed her by the arms and held her in place. "We can't give ourselves away! There'll be no one to rescue them."

Abby groaned. "Those dirty varmints."

"At least we know where he is," Luke said, releasing her.

Abby turned to him, her face ashen. "But where's Sarah?" Feeling faint, she grabbed Luke's arm for support.

Just then Bernie rose and stretched. His shirt came untucked, and his belly popped out when he scratched his chest. Leaving the rifle on the chair, he picked up a bull hide whip, raised it high, and cracked it wickedly through the air over the children's heads. They all crouched lower. Abby saw Kini jump with shock, then drop his pan in the river. He looked up in fear and lunged to retrieve it—and as he did, Abby saw Sarah's corn silk blonde hair beside him! He'd been blocking her view of precious Sarah. Abby gasped with relief, and Luke winked at her.

Bernie strode down a few paces to Kini and stood above him in the ankle-deep water. He gripped Kini by the hair and pulled him up to a standing position.

"You stupid kid! Don't drop the gold again! Give me what you got."

Luke and Abby watched Kini take off a leather pouch hanging from his neck and hand it over. The kidnapper hefted it to feel its weight. "Not enough!" he roared, and Kini shrank back. Little Sarah's face was stricken with fear. Abby gripped Luke's shoulder in a death grip, her fingernails digging in for fear she'd leap from the trees and yell at the beast!

"Ouch!" Luke said. "Come on, let's get out of here before we do something stupid."

He grabbed Abby by the hand and pulled her from the trees and back the way they'd come. Abby stared after Sarah as long as she could.

When they were some distance away, Luke spoke gently. "Don't worry, Abby. We'll free them tomorrow. If God can rescue me from a raging bear, He can help us rescue Sarah and Kini."

Abby knew he was right, but it hurt to leave the kids there. They had to set up camp and make plans for tomorrow's rescue. But, oh, how she longed to charge in and save Sarah and Kini right this minute!

Luke and Abby backtracked to the little glade by the stream where he'd camped the night before. While he built a fire, Abby investigated the old weathered rowboat on the shore. She bent over and grabbed a handful of the rotting fishing nets heaped in the bottom. "Yuck!" she hollered. They smelled like dead fish.

Soon a fire was blazing, and Luke's one pan was bubbling with water and tea. They shared his tin cup to sip from along with jerky and rock-hard biscuits. They talked for hours, each coming up with ideas, but none of them foolproof.

Finally, late into the night, Luke fell asleep in his blanket. On the other side of the campfire, Abby lay back, Sweet Pea's blanket wrapped around her. Crickets chirped and the frogs along the creek bed chorused back. *Re-deep, re-deep.* Abby was desperately tired, but her mind wouldn't let her rest. If only Duncan were here, she felt sure his prayers would move God's hand and everything would work out tomorrow.

Dear God, she prayed silently, *send Duncan to our rescue! Help him find us—right now!*

Above the chorus of frogs and the river's song, Abby heard God's voice. YOU PRAY WITH FAITH, came the gentle but firm command.

Abby gasped and sat up. *Me? My prayers could be enough?*

WITHOUT FAITH IT IS IMPOSSIBLE TO PLEASE GOD. ONE MUST ASK BELIEVING, AND NOT DOUBT.

Abby swallowed hard. *Of course, God can do anything. Of course, I know that—and I should believe that as I pray.* With new hope in her heart, she prayed, *God, I know You can do anything. Please, please help us rescue my sister and Kini tomorrow. Give us a good plan. I know if You are with us, we will succeed.*

Abby lay back down, her soul no longer in turmoil and fear. She knew God could do this for her and that He'd even inspired her to have more faith!

The moon floated silently overhead, and for a while Abby watched it sail through the pine trees.

That's when the idea struck. Sailing. Boats. The old weathered rowboat on the shore! A plan was taking shape. The stinky nets kept coming to mind, and suddenly she remembered her wonderful Hawaiian friend Olani and how she'd once used nets to outsmart a villain.

When Luke began to snore, Abby could swear a nearby bullfrog answered him.

She brought Ma's scented handkerchief from her pocket to her face and breathed in the now-faint scent of lilacs. "God's going to help me get Sarah back tomorrow, Ma," she whispered. "And Kini, too."

Abby heard a scratching sound on tree bark nearby.

Lord, I hate to bother You again, but since You're going to help me with the big things, could You please help me with a little thing, too? I'd be grateful if You'd keep the crawling critters away tonight! Amen.

Abby woke to find the dark night giving way to shades of gray. Even as she watched, the stars seemed to be winking out one by one. She yawned and rose, already dressed. Grabbing the frying pan, she went to the creek and filled it with water.

Then she fed leaves, twigs, and a log onto the dying embers. Soon a cheery blaze was going. Abby woke Luke with a nudge. "I've got a plan," she said.

Luke rolled over and grunted. "Can it wait till the sun's up?" he begged.

"Nope, rise and shine. We've got to set the captives free!" Luke's eyes popped open, and he tossed back his blanket. Over a shared cup of tea and bread, the two began to discuss Abby's plan.

"It's dangerous," Abby said, "but it just might work." Luke leaned forward eagerly.

Chapter Fourteen

"The important thing," Abby said, "is that I take care of one of the kidnappers, so you only have one to deal with."

"The problem is timing," Luke said. "If we each had a pocket watch, then we'd know exactly when to go into action." He pushed a hand through his blond-streaked hair in frustration.

"That's true." Abby finished braiding her hair and tied it with string. "I'll have to find a place a little upstream so I can see you coming before they do—and somehow get out and remounted before you arrive."

"All right," Luke said, "it's sunup . . . no doubt they've already unchained the kids and put them to work."

Abby shuddered at the thought of little Sarah knee-deep in that icy water in the cold morning air.

Luke gave her a leg up on Sweet Pea, then went over to the rowboat and pushed it into the river while hanging on to its rope. "Follow me until I get situated on the bank upstream, then head back toward the cabin and get ready to distract those snakes. I'll give you forty minutes or so."

He paused and looked Abby in the eye. "Whatever you do, don't get caught! I won't feel too good about getting the others away if you're left behind!"

Abby crouched in the same hiding place she'd been in the day before. From here she could see the cabin, the clearing, and the river beyond.

There was no time to lose. The children were already panning gold. Bernie sat in his chair, looking bored. Gordo was a bit upstream. Abby slipped silently through the woods behind the cabin and took up her lookout post near a bend in the river. Sweet Pea was tied to a bush near the cabin, but out of sight.

Abby's palms grew slick as she waited for Luke to come sailing down the rushing river in the old weathered boat. He had a long pole to guide it, but what if it was going too fast and sped by the children? Or if it went too slow, so Luke got caught? It had to go just right.

Worse yet, she had to run quickly once she sighted Luke so she could remount Sweet Pea and do her part. Abby lamented once again that she'd inherited her ma's weak legs. She ran as slow as a turtle. Her heart pounded in nervous anticipation.

O God, help us!

Luke walked the weathered rowboat out into the river. He had tied a rope to it and pulled it down the stream with Abby until it merged with the larger river. From there they'd progressed on foot along the bank until he'd decided they'd come close enough. Then Abby had headed out to do her part.

Now Luke pushed the boat into the cold, clear waters of the American River. It felt icy, the current strong with the river full and rushing after winter rains. If he timed it right, Abby's diversion would draw one of the cutthroats away from the kids at just the right moment. He'd be responsible for the other one.

He laid the long birch pole he'd hacked with his pickax across the gunwales and climbed in quickly. Taking his pole, he pushed off against the river-bed. The rowboat had no oars, so the pole would have to do. *This whole venture is one big risk,* he thought grimly. *But without a gun, what choice do we have?*

The river caught the boat like a fallen leaf, and it began its journey rapidly downstream toward the kidnappers.

Abby had no sooner prayed when Luke's face came into view as the boat floated past the bend in the river and headed toward Gordo and Bernie. She turned and sprinted as fast as possible toward the cabin and Sweet Pea. Her heart thudded against her ribs, and her stomach lurched toward her throat.

She ran without concern for the sound of her footsteps or heavy breathing. *Umph!* She went sprawling over a tree root she hadn't seen. "Ouch!" She pushed herself off the ground and went on, skinned knees and all. *I've got to rescue Sarah and Kini!*

She skittered to a stop beside Sweet Pea and ripped the reins out of the bush. Leading the gentle horse to a tree stump, Abby tried to mount, but the mare began to walk back toward the bush she'd been nibbling. "No!" Abby yanked the reins and pulled her to the stump again. The horse set her ears back in irritation but held still this time as Abby threw one leg over.

Now she was on, and there was no time to lose! Already she heard a shout from one of the men. *They've seen Luke!*

She punched her heels into Sweet Pea's sides, and the horse leapt forward. Abby passed the cabin and headed straight toward Bernie, who stood with his back to her, the bullwhip raised high in his right hand. As Abby watched, he whipped it over the children's heads as he'd done yesterday. It shrieked through the air, and a cry went up from the children as they all ducked.

It was just what Abby needed to prompt her. Anger surged through her, and she wished for the biggest peppershaker in the world to whack this varmint on the head, like she had once done to her enemy, Jackal. Instead, she gathered the smelly fishnet draped over Sweet Pea's neck and held it in both hands. She clung with her knees to the mare, urging her toward Bernie, the turkey gobbler.

She'd seen caballeros do something like this with wild calves, only they'd used lariats. Hers was a lariat of sorts, only with a net attached to it. As Bernie raised his arm again to whip the children into submission, Abby held the net aloft. At the last instant, Bernie heard the horse hooves and turned, surprise lighting his face. His arm never had time to lash out at Abby, for she threw the net out and over his head and arm, then jerked the attached rope hard.

The net closed over his chest and pulled his arms in close to his torso. Abby guided Sweet Pea around him once, then twice, pulling the rope hard enough to knock him down. As soon as he hit the dirt, she screamed out, "Sarah!"

She kneed Sweet Pea, who cantered toward the

river. Sarah's eyes grew wide the second she saw Abby. She dropped her pan and leapt through the icy water to shore, where Sweet Pea stood. Abby reached out a hand, adrenaline coursing through her, and yanked Sarah up behind her as if she weighed nothing. In that split second, with Sarah gripping her waist for dear life, Abby realized how much she loved her irritating little sister.

"I knew you'd come!" Sarah shouted as she clung to Abby's back. Abby almost cried with relief until she turned Sweet Pea and saw that Bernie was wriggling free of his net! The look of surprise on his face had changed to one of pure hatred. Abby knew in her gut that he wanted nothing more than to capture her and add her to his slave laborers—or he just might be content to kill her!

"Giddyap!" Abby ordered, and Sweet Pea sprang into action.

Abby glanced over to Kini, who was grinning at her rescue attempts. "Luke's coming!" she hollered, motioning frantically upriver. Kini turned and caught sight of the boat.

But at the same instant, so did Gordo. He began wading out to intercept the boat skimming toward Kini and the others.

Abby knew she had done her part. Now as she turned the mare downstream, away from the cutthroats, she glanced over her shoulder just in time to see Bernie up and lunging for Sarah's leg!

As the boat sailed quickly past Gordo, Luke began yelling. "Kini, get in! Get in, kids! It's time to escape!" He frantically leaned toward Kini as the boat rushed downriver. The children would have to wade out deeper to catch the boat.

Apparently Gordo got the drift of what was happening and threw himself into the icy waters in an effort to stop Luke. He dog-paddled toward the boat even as Kini urged everyone toward the oncoming vessel. "Come!" he yelled.

Luke stuck the pole into the river and pushed the boat toward shore while Kini and the children splashed toward him. The largest Indian boy tried to hold the boat as it came within reach, but the current was tugging it from his clutches. Luke leapt from the boat into waist-deep water and held it against the swirling tide. In seconds, all the children climbed aboard.

Suddenly Gordo was upon them, aiming blows on Luke. But Luke managed to throw himself against Gordo and knock him off his feet. As the kidnapper submerged, Luke dove after the drifting boat and, with Kini's help, hauled himself in. When he looked back, he saw that Gordo had gripped the rope that trailed behind the boat. The snake was being dragged along with them and was moving hand over fist to get to them!

Too late, Luke spotted Bernie chasing Abby and
Sarah on shore. He craned his neck to catch sight
between the locust trees that dotted the riverbank.
Even as he watched, the man rushed after the girls
and Sweet Pea. Now the snake had Sarah by the leg!
If he yanked her off the horse, no doubt Abby would
go after her. Then they'd both be caught for sure!

Unable to help her, Luke watched with a sinking
heart from the heavily laden rowboat as it floated
downstream, dragging Gordo.

"Let go!" Abby demanded. Fury surged through her
as Bernie lunged at Sarah and grabbed her leg. Abby
slapped him with the reins, but he didn't seem to
feel it. She could smell whiskey on his labored
breath as he struggled to pull Sarah from the horse.

Sweet Pea snorted and pranced sideways in fear,
her eyes wide, as Sarah's piercing scream rang out
again and again. Her grasp around Abby's waist
was loosening.

They moved toward the rushing river while Sweet
Pea snorted in terror. Suddenly the gentle mare
kicked out, and her hoof rocketed into Bernie's
stomach. Bernie's mouth formed an *O* as the air
whooshed out, and he went sailing backward. As he
splashed into the river, Abby quickly urged Sweet
Pea forward with a kick in her sides. "Giddyap!"

Even as the horse picked up her feet and
cantered down the riverbank, Abby and Sarah
looked over their shoulders. Bernie had already
risen from the river, water streaming from his
clothes, and was rushing for his rifle.

"Duck, Sarah!"

A shot rang out and echoed downriver.

Abby heard a tree limb above them crack.
As the girls galloped by, it fell with a splash in
the shallows. They rounded a bend, and Abby
breathed more easily since they were now out
of the rifle's range.

Sweet Pea dodged rocks and trees while
Abby searched to her right and caught sight
of the children piled in the rowboat. She could
see it was overloaded and might even sink in
the rushing waters. But that wasn't the biggest
problem.

"That bad man is hanging on!" Sarah screamed.

To her horror, Abby watched Gordo pulling
himself toward the stern of the boat by the trailing
rope. Then she saw Luke stand up in the stern of
the rocking craft and unsheathe his bowie knife.
He bent over the stern of the boat and toward the
rope. Abby knew that Luke planned to cut Gordo
free, but the villain must have thought the knife
was for him. He let go in a hurry and struck out
toward shore. Abby and Sarah galloped past him
just as he dragged himself like a wet cat out of the
river and collapsed.

Luke saw Abby and Sarah riding along the shore and waved. Abby could make out his dimple as he grinned broadly. "There are the girls that helped rescue you," he shouted to the children in the boat.

Abby and Sarah smiled and waved as the kids erupted in cheers and hollers. They would travel on for another few miles until they were out of reach of the kidnappers; then they would join up on the bank.

Chapter Fifteen

Twenty minutes later, Luke poled the boat toward the bank, where Abby and Sarah waited. When Kini climbed out of the weathered old boat and splashed through the shallows, Sarah threw her arms around him and bubbled, "Did you see Abby come to my rescue? Even Pa couldn't have done it better!"

Abby stood amazed at her sister's choice of words. She knew she had God to thank for their success.

Kini laughed happily and hugged Sarah back. When Abby turned to him, Kini laced his fingers together and held them up for her. "We be three strands of rope! When one friend falls down, other friend picks him up."

Abby hugged him tightly and nodded. As the excitement died down, the five Indian children, Kini, and Luke sat on the riverbank. Each took a piece of jerky and a biscuit from Abby, except Sarah, who clutched something in her hand.

"What is it, Sarah?" Abby questioned.

Sarah beamed as if she had a secret, then held up a leather bag on a string.

"Is that the kidnappers' gold?" Abby asked.

Sarah silently bent down and untied the knotted drawstring. She licked one finger and stuck it in. When she drew her finger out, gold dust stuck to it. "My foot got caught in the string when that bad man tried to yank me off the horse," she explained. "And when he went flying, it stayed on my foot. Then I grabbed it quick!"

"Good job, Little Britches!" Kini said. "You take what they be wanting most!"

Everyone laughed, then dug into their vittles. Between bites of food, the children grinned at one another. One lad almost as tall as Luke spoke in broken English. "We here one moon."

"Do you mean about a month?" Luke questioned. The lad nodded.

Three boys a bit older than Kini ate quickly, and Abby realized they were half starved. Most distressing was the skinny little boy who looked to be only seven or eight years old. He was so young to work all day as a slave.

Then she remembered the sad Indian couple and their missing son. "Are any of you called *Yano?*"

The youngest boy glanced up. "I . . . Yano," he said quietly.

Abby jumped up. "Your mother and father are searching for you. They'll be coming back to Coloma—and they'll be so happy to see you!"

146

Yano smiled shyly.

The oldest Indian boy spoke up. "I take others to parents. Our tribe in hills four days' journey from here. They go high up, where white men not go yet. I know way."

Abby and Luke exchanged glances. Luke motioned for the tall boy to walk downriver where they could talk.

When they came back ten minutes later, Luke said, "Zatos can take them. He does know the way, and we can give them the rest of our food to see them home."

Abby nodded. "But I think Yano should come with us. His parents said they would come back because I promised to ask around." Abby turned to Yano and asked him if he would be willing. The young boy's luminous brown eyes were eager. "We go now!" he urged.

Sarah got up and walked to Zatos, the oldest boy, as he gathered the three other Indian children into a circle around him. "This gold can buy supplies for your tribe," she explained.

Sarah, Abby, Luke, Kini, and Yano watched as the four Indian children raised their hands in a happy farewell. They waved until they disappeared among the distant trees. Then Abby, Sarah, and Yano mounted Sweet Pea with Luke and Kini chatting away by the mare's side as they began the long walk back to camp.

They had hiked three-fourths of the way back to Coloma when Abby drew up the reins and said to Luke, "Does that rider look familiar?"

Luke followed Abby's pointing finger. Coming down the last slope before they reached their campsite was a lone rider. "Luke," Abby said with excitement, "I think it's Duncan!"

Sure enough the rider cantering toward them wore a wide-brimmed hat and a black patch over his left eye. Luke hooted. "And he's on Lightning, my horse!"

In a minute Duncan was reining up beside Abby in a cloud of dust. Sarah threw out her arms, and Duncan leaned across his saddle horn to take her in his lap. "Little Brrritches, I surely missed ye!" He nuzzled her with his scratchy chin, and Sarah giggled and squirmed.

Turning to Luke and Abby, he shook his head and grinned. "So, 'tis another adventure fer the three o'ye?" He eyed the Indian child and smiled kindly. "Me name is Duncan, son. And who are ye?"

"I, Yano. Mother and Father come look for me."

Sarah couldn't stand it any longer. "Some bad men stole me and Kini, but Abby and Luke rescued us and the other kids!"

Duncan's eyebrow shot up, and he gazed at Abby. Sheepishly she admitted it was true. "And where are the varrrmints who stole these children in the first place?" he asked as he twirled his moustache. His eye had an angry gleam to it, which made Abby ever so happy.

"Up the river, nursing their wounded pride," Luke answered.

Duncan's one-eyed glare pierced Luke. "Can ye find their place again?"

"Easily," Luke answered.

"Good. I think we should pay them a visit. But first, let's get everyone safely back to camp. I know one storeowner who's beside herself with worry."

"Molly?" asked Abby.

"The same," Duncan answered, as they headed back to camp.

Once they arrived in camp, the children sat down to rest while Duncan led Sweet Pea to the mercantile to share the good news with Molly and John.

When Duncan returned to the children's camp with John and two other men, they had two extra horses.

"Luke," explained Duncan, "we'd like to go clean out that nest of snakes who think they can get away with kidnapping. Can ye lead us back?"

"Now?" Luke asked, exhausted and longing for a night of rest and food.

"Yes, son. I'd like to get them before they up and leave," Duncan answered. "And these good men have business to do tomorrow."

"Yes, sir," he said as he mounted the saddled horse.

"Don't worry, there's food aplenty," Duncan grinned. "Jerky and corn bread to yer heart's delight."

"Great," Luke said, trying to hide his disappointment. For the first time in a month, he thought of apples . . . shiny, red, juicy apples.

He'd have given ten dollars in gold for one bite.

Abby heard the men return to camp sometime during the middle of the night. She hurried out of the tent in her nightdress and coat and was delighted to see Gordo and Bernie hog-tied back-to-back on a horse. Bernie growled like a rabid dog when he saw Abby, but Duncan gave him a warning glance.

"Where are you taking them, Duncan?" she asked.

"To Mormon Island," he answered. "When I passed through a day ago, I met the jailer from Pueblo de San Jose. He'll be glad to have a few more convicts in chains panning for gold."

All the noise woke Sarah, who wandered out of the tent. Rubbing her eyes sleepily, she gazed up in astonishment at the kidnappers.

Gordo couldn't control himself, however. He cursed Abby and Sarah and tried to spit on them. Abby drew Sarah close and put a protective arm around her shoulder. From a safe distance, Sarah yelled at Gordo, "You're naughty! You need a mother very badly to teach you manners!"

Duncan and the others broke into chortles as they bid them good night. Sarah stumbled back to bed while Luke dismounted and handed another man his reins. "I'm off to bed," he announced. "Thanks again for the help, everyone."

Abby stopped him as he headed toward his tent. "Luke, are you ready to leave California?" Curls askew and eyes puffy from lack of sleep, she held her breath, anxiously awaiting his answer.

"There's nothing to stay for now, Abby. But I'd like to make one stop in Pueblo de San Jose before we leave for Hawaii."

Abby exhaled. "I'm so glad. I need to go home, Luke. Ma might need my help, and I think I have enough money now to pay Dr. Warbutton and maybe even buy the ranch."

Luke's eyes widened. "*You* have enough?"

She grinned in the light of the moon. "Haven't you heard of the Rich Diggin's Bakery? I've sold hundreds of pies and breads all month. And I have a boot full of gold nuggets and dust—and a little gold in the Coloma bank."

Luke whistled. "Well . . . I'll be. I can't ever seem

to get ahead of you, Abby. Truth is, I've learned I'd rather stay beside you anyway."

They grinned; then Luke turned again toward his tent.

Once back in her tent, it took Abby an hour to get back to sleep. Her mind raced with thoughts of leaving California and finally heading home. Would there be a letter waiting for her when they stopped in Pueblo de San Jose? And if there was, what news would it bring?

Abby got up and searched through her dress pocket. Then, grabbing the hankie, she pressed it to her face, barely catching any lilac scent at all now. She climbed back into bed. "Oh, Ma," she whispered as Sarah slept next to her, "we'll be seeing you soon. Please be well . . . please, please be there!"

When Duncan returned to camp later that morning, Abby asked him if he was planning on staying to mine gold.

"Nay, lassie. Let's pack up and get home!"

"But Duncan, don't you want to stay and make your fortune in the goldfields like everyone else?"

"Nay, I'm eager fer sailing on soft trade winds . . . fer the white sand and turquoise sea. And Abby, I confess I have a terrible hunger to discover what happened to me da. I'm heading to Hawaii to untangle the mystery that surrounds me father, if I can."

"You will, Duncan! I know it. Maybe Luke and I can help you." She gazed up with confidence at her one-eyed friend.

"I'd like that, lassie."

Chapter Sixteen

It never occurred to Abby to sell her business—
the makeshift table, oven, pie pans, supplies, and
tent. But that's just what she did when a young
widow with three children showed up the very next
morning. "My husband died on the trail out here,"
the pretty young woman explained. "I don't have
any other way to support myself, especially since I
still need to keep an eye on my young'uns." She
nodded at the baby in her arms and the two tiny
children clinging to her skirt. "I don't have any
money to buy your business. It all got ate up on
supplies, but maybe we could make a trade."

"What have you got?" Abby questioned.

"Only this pair of oxen and the wagon." Abby
examined the animals standing in the meadow. It
dawned on her that if she traded her business for
the wagon and oxen, she would not have to walk
twenty miles to the ferry landing. "Done!" Abby
held out her hand and the two shook.

"I declare," said the young widow, "I never
thought I would be running my own business! How
much do you reckon I can make in a month?"

Abby smiled at the eager face. "Over five hundred dollars, plus more if you bake breads."

The woman laughed. "You're a good jester. I'd be thrilled to claim that in a year."

"No, it's true!"

"Mercy," the widow said, catching her breath.

"This is a rare opportunity," Abby explained. "There will always be enough men to buy your pies and bread. And even if prices for flour and sugar keep rising, you can just raise your rates for pies. Besides that," Abby continued confidentially, "you'll love doing business with Molly and John from the mercantile."

The widow and her children promised to come back in two days' time to take possession of Abby's camp.

All Abby had to do now was haul her gold to Coloma and trade it in for gold coins. She was already busily at work, along with Luke and Sarah, sewing money belts, vests, and undergarments in which to hide the coins. No sense in getting robbed of all their hard work, not when the gold would do so much good at home in Hawaii.

Two days later the widow and her children reined in their oxen and began unloading their wagon. "You take the tarps covering the wagon ribs," Abby said. "We're on our way home and won't be needing them."

Meanwhile, Coyote had finally returned to claim his gear, having panned along the river on the way back, and had already left after hearing about a new strike to the east.

Just a day earlier, the Indian parents, Sopi and Toonatah, had returned in hopes that Abby had information about Yano. When they came into camp, Abby threw her arms around Sopi and told them the good news. But Yano and Kini had gone out hunting and wouldn't return for another hour.

When they finally did, with a fowl over Kini's back, Yano didn't immediately notice his parents. But Sopi clutched her heart and called out, "Son!"

Yano dropped his bow and raced to her. There were many tears of joy before the happy family took their leave with a small pouch of Abby's gold. Luke had insisted that Toonatah and his family travel to Pueblo de San Jose as soon as the baby was completely well and inquire about work at his aunt's ranch. "She's lost many *vaqueros*," he said, "and I'm sure she'll be glad to hire you." They promised they'd come.

Only Abby noticed the stricken look on Kini's face as he watched Yano's reunion and departure with his parents, which told her how much he missed his own family on Lanai.

Later that day, Duncan, Luke, Kini, Sarah, and Abby loaded their combined gold onto Lightning and hiked into Coloma and the newly formed bank. The bank manager meticulously weighed each ounce of gold on a fancy large scale that had just arrived from San Francisco. They exchanged their pile of gold nuggets and dust for shiny gold coins and returned to camp to pack up. One small trunk was full of gold coins, but the rest were distributed on everyone in money belts.

Abby, Luke, and Duncan also wore vests in which the gold coins were sewn into pockets lining the entire undergarment. The vests were heavy, and Abby was glad she wouldn't have to walk all the way to the ferry with it on. They would ride in the wagon, sell it and the oxen at the port city, and ferry Luke's horse, Lightning, back to Pueblo de San Jose with them.

After handing over all her cooking gear to the widow, Abby breathed a happy sigh. They were free to go. Abby took only her "Rich Diggin's Bakery" sign as a memento of her California business and, of course, her journal with drawings of Molly, John, and Yano. She had already said a tearful good-bye to Molly and John Sampson, who had grown so dear to her during her stay in Coloma, and they promised to write.

Now Abby, Luke, Sarah, and Kini climbed into the wagon, with Duncan on Lightning.

"Giddyap," Luke commanded the oxen with a gentle slap of the reins. The lumbering beasts stepped forward into their yoke, and the wagon began to creak and roll. Molly and John stood at the edge of the meadow and waved.

"Good-bye!" Abby called as the wagon jostled across the field of blue lupine and golden poppies.

"Good-bye goldfield adventure!" Sarah yelled.

Three days of travel finally brought them to the sleepy pueblo of San Jose. Abby and Sarah had ridden the horse most of the way from Alviso Landing. Now Abby got down as they entered town and let Kini take her place so she could walk next to Luke.

"We have to stop right away at Dr. Warbutton's," she said. "That way, while we're at your aunt's, he can be packing up to leave for Hawaii."

Luke's expression was unreadable. "I hope so, Abby."

Their boots made hollow sounds on the board-walk in front of Dr. Warbutton's office. Abby gripped the knob and turned it, letting herself into the dim interior that smelled of herbs. All of her hard work was bound to pay off now.

Dr. Warbutton looked up from his desk, strewn with papers and books. He pushed his glasses up his nose. "Well, young lady, what can I do for you?"

"Do you remember me?" Abby asked, aware that Luke stood right behind her. "I've returned from the goldfields, Dr. Warbutton, and I've brought you several hundred dollars to convince you to move to Hawaii with me!" Abby grinned with eager anticipation at the white-coated physician as he stood and came toward her.

"Ah, you young people are always joshing these days," he said with a chuckle.

Confused, Abby queried, "Oh . . . You want to see the gold first, right? May I use your examining room?"

The doctor turned curious eyes to Luke for an explanation. But Luke only shrugged.

Several seconds later Abby returned with her money belt in hand. She handed it to the doctor, who opened it and gasped at the sight of many gleaming gold dollars.

"Why, you weren't joshing me!" The doctor's head jerked up in astonishment at Abby.

"No, doctor, I earned that money to set you up in Hawaii. Can you leave tomorrow with us?"

Compassion stole across the doctor's aging features. "My dear girl, I can't leave Pueblo de San Jose. This is where I'm settling for the rest of my days. My family is here. I am so sorry I misunderstood you—and you me." He shook his head sadly and handed the money belt back to her.

Abby almost didn't take it back. She had been so convinced he would come. But Luke put a hand on her shoulder and steered her toward the door.

"Thanks for your time, doctor," he said, as he herded Abby out into the sunlight.

She walked on in misery. She'd failed again. All that work had been for nothing! Dr. Warbutton had never meant to come along . . . never meant to set up shop and help her ma.

She trudged on in pained silence for a while. Soon she and Luke caught up with the others who were laughing and talking about their adventures. But Abby's mind was not on their conversation. She was remembering how she so recently had felt like a failure—when Sarah was kidnapped—but God had turned it around for her. *YOU PRAY WITH FAITH,* He had told her.

Luke, who was walking beside her, took her hand in his own strong one and gave it a squeeze. Abby turned grateful eyes to his. Hiking out of town, she prayed with all the faith she had.

Chapter Seventeen

"Are you worried about seeing your aunt?" Abby asked, noticing Luke had grown quiet.

They had reached the lane that led to Dagmar Gronen's mansion. Abby held little hope that Luke's aunt would willingly let him go to Hawaii. After hearing why the children had left, Duncan said he would not force Luke to stay. But for some reason, Luke had insisted on saying good-bye.

"I'm not worried, Abby," Luke said as he thoughtfully swung a stick and tossed it over the dirt road they were traveling. "Ever since I talked to God, I've had peace in here." He tapped on his chest. "I just want a chance to tell her I . . . care about her. I keep thinking that maybe she feels as lonely as I have at times. I'd like to mend things if possible. But that's up to God. I've been praying for His help, though."

Abby gazed at his profile. She'd never felt so proud of anyone before.

Once again they walked down the lane of oak

trees, this time in daylight. They passed the corral, barn, and bunkhouse on the right. Once again Luke climbed the porch steps alone and knocked on the door.

He waited a long time before the door creaked open. But it wasn't Maria who greeted him. It was Mrs. Gronen, answering her own door!

"Aunt Dagmar," Luke began, stepping back a bit in surprise, "I've come back to . . . say good-bye."

Slowly the door opened and Mrs. Gronen said sternly, "Come in . . . all of you, come in."

Abby and Duncan eyed each other but then joined Luke on the porch. After Duncan and the children had filed cautiously into the house, Mrs. Gronen ordered, "Come to the kitchen."

She looked the same, Abby thought, but something was different. Gazing about the pretty parlor, Abby noticed a layer of dust coating the tables and bookcases. Unread newspapers littered the floor. The house was utterly quiet.

"Where's Maria?" Luke asked as they entered the once-tidy kitchen. The counters were littered with dirty dishes.

"Sit down," Mrs. Gronen ordered, and they all obeyed. "Maria left with her cousin's family two weeks ago. She was the last . . . to go. They have all left me for the goldfields."

Luke stared in astonishment. "Do you mean you're making your own meals, Aunt?"

Mrs. Gronen took a deep breath. "Yes, indeed."

She raised her nose an inch. "I am managing better than I expected. Except for the cows. But I hired Mr. Worley to take care of the stock."

"Jacob's grandfather?" Luke asked in astonishment.

"Yes, yes. And I am lucky to have him." Aunt Dagmar pursed her lips. "I can hardly believe the whole town has come down with gold fever. But there you have it. It has changed everything. With everyone so sure they will be rich next week, my wealth does not . . ."

Abby watched Mrs. Gronen swallow painfully.

"My wealth does not seem to matter anymore," Mrs. Gronen finally finished. The room was so still that Abby could hear the ticking of the regulator clock until Mrs. Gronen went on, tucking a frizzy gray lock back into her bun. "It is enough to give one a headache. But still, I am proud of the fact that Mr. Worley and I have managed to keep body and soul together entirely on our own. He is living here, you know, in the bunkhouse—until the world comes back to its senses and people want real jobs again!"

Mrs. Gronen sniffed and went to the pantry. "I just made this bread this morning. Mr. Worley insists that it is my best so far." She laid it on the kitchen counter with a hard thump. Taking a knife, she began sawing it.

Duncan caught Abby's eyes and raised an eyebrow. The sawing was taking some time.

Luke jumped up and offered to help. "Yes, indeed," Mrs. Gronen said. "You can get some of the milk that Mr. Worley brought in this morning and serve your friends."

Luke did so, then served each one a piece of bread as well. It was lucky they had the milk to soften the bread, or teeth would have shattered. Luke suppressed a grin as he said, "That's mighty interesting bread, Aunt Dagmar."

"Aye," Duncan agreed, "'tis bound to put hair on yer chest."

Mrs. Gronen actually smiled, and Abby was stunned. The woman looked completely different— human, in fact!

Well, I'll be! Abby thought. *Mrs. Gronen's riches made her feel like the most powerful person in these parts. No wonder she was arrogant and took everyone for granted. But the gold rush has changed all that. Looks like some honest work has helped her see that she needs others. Why, it's even made her appreciate people—like Luke—more!*

"Aunt," Luke began, "I've been planning on going back to Hawaii with Abby and the others. But I can see you're in a pickle, what with the help all leaving."

Mrs. Gronen joined them at the table. Fixing her steely gaze on Luke, she questioned, "Why did you leave the goldfields?"

"I learned gold isn't half as important as friendship, and it'll never compare with the treasure of God's love."

Mrs. Gronen seemed stunned by Luke's answer. Her lips twitched for a few seconds, as if she couldn't speak.

Luke cleared his throat. "I came back to tell you, Aunt, that I care about you. If you need me to stay until you can find another worker or two, I will. In fact, I've sent one to you—his name is Toonatah, and he should be arriving within the week."

Abby waited anxiously for Mrs. Gronen's reaction. The widow's head came up and she nodded. "I see you have gained quite an education in the goldfields, young man." She assessed him for a moment. "You have the look of my brother—your father—about you more and more. But no, Luke, I think Mr. Worley and I shall do all right. It was thoughtful of you to send a worker my way. I appreciate your offer, but I can see you want to go. And . . . now I understand why."

Luke took a deep breath. "Thank you, Aunt Dagmar."

"Well," she continued, "there are plenty of bedrooms for all of you. If you are starting on your journey tomorrow, you will need a good night's sleep. Although I expect you all to help me wash the sheets before you leave!"

As if in a daze, they followed Mrs. Gronen to their respective bedrooms. "No more barns!" Kini whispered happily to Abby before she moved down the hall with Sarah.

When Sarah entered the same room they'd slept in before, Abby followed Mrs. Gronen back into the hall. "Have you by any chance received a letter from my pa?"

"Indeed, but I had forgotten until you asked." Mrs. Gronen turned and rustled down the hall in her black silk dress, motioning for Abby to follow.

Abby's insides suddenly felt queasy as she followed Mrs. Gronen down the stairs to the desk in the parlor. The widow opened her oak rolltop and searched through a few envelopes. She extracted one from the pile and handed it to Abby. "You may sit here by the lamp and read it," Mrs. Gronen said as she headed back up the stairs, leaving Abby alone.

Abby stood frozen, staring at the writing. It was Pa's. *Does that mean Ma is not well enough to write, or Ma can't write?* Abby's heart sped up as she carefully ripped open the back and took out a single sheet of paper.

24 April 1848

Dearest Abby,
Little by little your mother is recovering from her mysterious fever. Although she is weak, you will be happy to hear she sits in the sun each day and says that it, and the good Lord, are

*restoring her to health. We have much to praise
Him for!*

Tears blurred Abby's vision as she read on,
hungry for more.

*Naturally, we are eager to hear about you,
Sarah, Kini, and Luke—and how you are faring
at Mrs. Gronen's home. No doubt you will be
quite spoiled by the time you get back, what with
all the servants waiting on you hand and foot!
But truth be told, I could really use your help
here with the chores. I didn't realize until now
how much your mother and I depend on you.*

*Do not write back—just catch the next avail-
able ship home. Your mother, Uncle Samuel,
and I sorely miss you all.*

*With deep affection,
Your loving father, Thomas Kendall*

The words swam before Abby's eyes as she stared
at the letter. When she heard the front door open,
she wiped away her tears. Duncan entered and
towered over her. "Abby," he questioned, his voice
full of compassion, "what is it, lassie?"

Too choked up to speak, Abby threw herself into
the Scotsman's arms. "Ma's all right," she finally
whispered against his neck.

Duncan held her fast. "Praise the Almighty!" he

thundered, forgetting that some had already gone to bed. "Oh, lassie, I'm rrrejoicing with ye."

When Abby showed him the part in the letter about her getting spoiled, she and Duncan threw back their heads and belly-laughed.

Chapter Eighteen

Two days later Duncan and the kids stood near the newly erected dock of San Francisco. Amid the seagull cries and the swirling mists just breaking up at noon came the constant sound of hammers. The sleepy little port city was being built before their eyes. At least a hundred ships floated in the bay, "with more arriving every day," one merchant had told them. Many businesses had been abandoned as tradesmen, doctors, and lawyers rushed to the fabled goldfields.

But as thousands of new people arrived, some looked at the opportunities to be had right here. Most of the ships in the bay, which were anchored to the seabed, had been abandoned. Whole crews had rushed toward riches. "How are we going to sail home?" Abby asked in anguish. "There's no one leaving!"

Duncan shook his head. "Let's not worry about it today, lassie. We've just arrived. Let's find food and ask where to stay the night." With that he herded them toward the street that fronted the bay. Many new shops had sprung up to accommodate the flood of arrivals. Everyone was looking for mining gear and supplies.

Soon they came upon a unique restaurant. Once a sailing ship, it had recently been towed to shore and converted into a place to eat. It was so crowded they had to wait their turn for a table. Standing in line behind them was a man dressed in a blue wool seaman's jacket. The fine brass buttons and braid on it set Abby to thinking.

She turned and introduced herself. "Would you happen to be a ship's captain?" she asked.

"Why I am that, young woman," the middle-aged man responded. "My name is Captain Smallwood. But why do you ask?"

"We've just returned from the goldfields and need to sail to Hawaii. But we can't find any vessels that are leaving."

Captain Smallwood laughed. "I shouldn't wonder. I know of two *kanakas* who want to go home to the islands, too. They care little for riches, but no one else wants to miss this opportunity. My crew jumped ship a day ago, and I am bound for Coloma myself." When the captain asked Abby and her party about their experiences there, Luke shared his story about the rich vein he'd found in his dry diggings.

The captain was so tickled with the news of easy gold that he rubbed his salt-and-pepper beard with a gleam in his eye. "I'll be generous back," he said.

"My ship, the *Fair Winds,* lies yonder in the bay."
He pointed her out. "She's a sixty-eight-foot schooner—small, but she handles like a dream. I know
she'll rot or be ripped to pieces for the lumber
before I return. But by then I won't care. I'll be
rich! You take her," he said to Duncan. "Sail her
to the islands. You've no other way to get home,
and all I ask as payment is a little gold and a map
to those dry diggings you've told me about." He
waited while Luke's mouth gaped open.

"Your whole ship for a hand-drawn map and
some gold?" Luke asked.

"Yes, and I've left all my navigational charts and
equipment aboard. Everything in fact—my library
of fine books and a dozen barrels of water, salted
fish, and flour. I can't carry them with me. But can
you sail, man?" the captain asked, pinning Duncan
with his stare.

"Yes," Duncan answered, "but I can't just take
her, sir. If ye'll take some payment and give me a
bill of sale, I'll buy her."

Captain Smallwood put out his hand. "It's a
deal. Five twenty-dollar gold pieces will help me
buy mining gear—and I need the map." Duncan
handed over his own gold pieces to Captain Smallwood, who quickly wrote out a bill of sale for the
Fair Winds, formerly of Nantucket Island. Duncan
stored the paper in his vest pocket.

"Now," the captain concluded, "take my advice
and seek out those two *kanakas* I told you about.

Hawaiians are the best seamen in the world, and they will do you a world of good. I last saw them sitting on the new pier, looking for a way home."

"Duncan," Abby said eagerly, "we should search for them now, don't you think?"

Duncan's one gray eye lit up with excitement. "I agrrree, lassie. Let's go." As they left the line and headed back toward the new pier, Duncan explained that he'd learned how to navigate on his sail across the Atlantic, but he'd prefer to have some experienced sailors onboard.

"Even with two *kanakas,* 'twill be a small crew, and 'twill be hard. No one will have much sleep, but it seems Providence has given us this, and no other way, to get home."

Abby walked quickly to keep up with the others while analyzing the "crew" around her. Luke was as tall and strong as a man. And she could haul sheets and swab the deck as well as cook the meals. Kini knew how to climb coconut trees, so rigging couldn't be much worse. Sarah could certainly annoy them all, thus keeping them awake.

Yes, perhaps it could be done! "Let's find those homesick sailors," she begged, "and go home."

They paid for bread, cheese, and apples at a stand and hurried down to the wharf. It didn't take long to locate the two burly Hawaiian sailors, Kai and Liho. They eagerly agreed to join up and spoke in Hawaiian to Kini, who grinned enthusiastically at the turn of events.

The *kanakas* knew the *Fair Winds* and rowed Duncan, Sarah, and Kini out to the ship. Abby and Luke volunteered to stay onshore and buy supplies for the trip with some of Abby's gold. The sailors would be back to pick her and Luke up in two hours at the wharf.

Abby sat on a barrel in front of Bishop Mercantile. The late-afternoon sun warmed her as a cooling sea breeze came in off the nearby bay. Luke had gone around back to borrow a hand-drawn cart which the store owner was willing to lend them, seeing as they'd spent so much money on supplies. In her boredom, she glanced down the wooden boardwalk to the other stores. A young boy sat three stores down, tending something in a wooden crate. She could see him talking to whatever was inside. Curious, she got up and wandered over.

As she neared the young boy, she called out, "What are you selling?"

The boy, only ten or so, gave her a grin. "Puppies! The best pups in the West," he said with the conviction of a true salesman.

Excitement shot through Abby. *If only they are a little like Sparks,* she thought, *I could surprise Luke with one! He's missed his dog so much.*

She hurried forward. The fluffy balls of fur were

part collie, like Sparks, and part yellow Lab. Abby cooed with delight as she bent down and picked one up. Its little pink tongue immediately came out and licked her cheek, and she giggled. "Puppy breath!" she said fondly. Squatting, she set the puppy down to watch it walk. "How old are they?"

"Eight weeks old," the boy replied proudly. "They come from good stock, too."

"Is this one a girl?" Abby asked.

The boy picked up the yellow-and-white pup and checked. "Yep, sure is. She'll make a good mother someday, just like my dog."

Abby nodded. "I'll take her!" She quickly handed over a coin in payment. But no sooner had she done so than the puppy, who'd been sniffing the boards, went trotting off and disappeared through an open door a few feet away. Abby hopped up and chased her.

She stepped through the doorway and called softly, "Here, puppy . . ."

As soon as her eyes adjusted to the dim light, she saw the frisky little canine crawling under a desk, chasing a dust ball.

Abby glanced up and met the curious stare of a clean-shaven young man. "Hello," he said, "have you lost something?"

She grinned. "My new puppy's run under your desk." The smiling stranger bent down and picked the pup up, holding her aloft for Abby. "Thanks," she said, taking her and cuddling her against her chest.

As she was turning to leave she couldn't help but notice folded clothes and a variety of labeled bottles spread out on a nearby table. Half-packed boxes were strewn about the place.

She turned back to the friendly man. "Are you a doctor?"

He glanced up from his packing. "Yes, I am. Dr. Sheldon Armstrong, at your service," he said with a wink. "Does your puppy need my services?"

Abby giggled. "No . . . but I can't help but wonder where you are going, Dr. Armstrong."

"Oh, that's easy to answer. To the goldfields!"

Abby sighed. "It seems everyone's catching gold fever," she said sadly.

"Gold fever?" he questioned. He closed the box he'd been working on and gave her his full attention.

"You must have a case of gold fever to be heading to Coloma," Abby said.

"No," he replied, grinning. "Not me. But all my patients do. That's why I'm leaving. The city's cleaning out. Most of my patients have already left." He grabbed an empty box and began settling in the bottles between stacks of rags. "I'm just heading to the gold country so I can do what I love best—practice medicine."

Abby's palms grew moist with excitement. "Dr. Armstrong, if you love to practice medicine, I know a place where you'll surely be appreciated—not to mention desperately needed!" She went on to explain that there were no doctors on her side of Oahu, but enough people to make it worth his while. "And I can give you free passage on our ship, which is leaving with the morning light!" Abby paused. "Umm, I do hope you won't mind helping with the sail, Dr. Armstrong. We are a small crew."

The young doctor began to smile. "I don't mind at all. And I believe your puppy was sent by Providence! I've always wanted to go to the Pacific Isles . . . imagine a free—er, a working—trip!"

When Abby, with left hand wrapped about the squirming puppy, stuck out her right hand, Dr. Armstrong shook it vigorously. They quickly made plans to meet on the pier at dawn's first light.

Abby sailed from Dr. Armstrong's office on a cloud of joy, only to be met by a frowning best friend. "Where have you been?" Luke asked testily.

"Finding your runaway puppy!" she said happily, as she thrust the furry bundle into Luke's arms. When the pup's pink tongue came out and licked his fingers, Luke's face dimpled with delight.

"Abby, I love it!"

"It's a her," she clarified. "What are you going to name her?"

Luke held the puppy at arm's length while she squirmed in his hands. "Hmm, she's blonde like . . . Hawaii's sandy beaches. I'm going to call her

'Sandy,'" he said as he brought her snugly back against his chest.

Sandy's little tail flipped back and forth happily, and Abby grinned. "I think she likes her new name. And her new owner." She took Sandy from Luke and nodded at the loaded cart. "You pull and I'll carry," she said. As they hiked back to the pier, she quickly explained her good news of finding a doctor willing to move to Kailua.

Their two new Hawaiian friends were waiting to row them to their new home, the *Fair Winds*. As they loaded the dinghy, Abby wondered about Duncan's reaction to their four-footed addition. But she didn't have to wait long, for they rowed out to the ship quickly.

As they came alongside the rope ladder, Duncan greeted them. "Ahoy, lassie and laddies!" he called out cheerfully. "Welcome aboard."

Then he looked down at Abby and groaned. "What have ye done, lassie? Are ye in love with the dog?"

"Oh, it's not for me, Duncan; she belongs to Luke. But I admit, I bought her to cheer him up. Before we discuss the dog," Abby said hopefully, "I want to tell you I found another hand to help with the sail."

For a moment, the good news seemed to take the starch out of Duncan's bluster. "Well, 'tis good news." Then he continued, scowling, "But a dog . . . on deck? 'Twill make a mess!"

Abby gave him a mischievous smile as she climbed the rope ladder and clambered on deck. She bent down to retrieve the puppy from Luke and thrust the plump, soft-furred creature in Duncan's arms. It settled into the crook of his elbow and licked his wrist. He sighed. "Oh, me bonnie ship . . ."

Suddenly Sarah showed up at the railing, screaming with delight. The puppy barked a little "woof," and Sarah took her from Duncan and squeezed her.

"I will allow it on one condition," Duncan said sternly. He pinned Abby and Luke with an ominous stare. "The deck is to be swabbed frequently, if ye get me meanin'. Are ye agrrreed?"

Abby leaned up on tiptoe and kissed him on the cheek. "Yes, Duncan. Whatever you say."

Dinner was a happy affair. They sat in the swaying galley, oil lamp burning brightly, as they shared Duncan's chicken stew.

Afterward Abby asked Luke to retrieve the brass tub they'd seen. She half filled it with warmed seawater and saw to it that Sarah gave herself a good scrubbing. Then Abby rinsed her with a bucket of fresh water. After Sarah was in bed, Abby had her own delicious bath. Her long hair swirled in the

steamy water, and she scrubbed with a new bar
of lilac soap.

It was heavenly preparation for a wonderful
sleep. The ship rocked gently; the mists closed in
and muted the sounds of waves on the shore.

When Abby fell into her bunk with its pillow
and warm quilt, she slept soundly beside Sarah.

Duncan rang the ship's bell before the sun even rose.

Kai rowed to the dock and picked up Dr.
Armstrong with his sixteen boxes of worldly and
medical goods. And the happy-go-lucky doctor
immediately fit in with the crew like he was family.

Kai, Liho, Abby, and Luke handled the sails as Kini
and Dr. Armstrong stood at the wheel, taking orders
from Duncan. It took them quite a while to master
the lines and rigging for the first week of sailing, but
before long, things settled into a routine. When
things were hectic on deck, Sarah did her part by
keeping Sandy, the puppy, out of harm's way.

Luke stayed awake on watch more than anyone
but Duncan, who was enchanted with his new
home. Sandy followed at Luke's heels wherever he
went, and she was smart enough to stay away from
the ship's railing. The puppy always lay in Luke's
berth with him, her head upon his chest or snuggled
against his neck.

The first week merged into two on the open sea.
Thankfully the weather was fair and the breezes held
steady. "We're making good progress," Duncan
confided to Abby one afternoon as she sat in the
sunny stern of the ship, drawing a picture of Luke
at the wheel.

Duncan continued. "Kai tells me we should make
Oahu in the next ten days." Since settling in on the
ship, they had all pulled together as a team. Even
Sarah agreed readily to her share of work, but there
was still time for fun and games, too.

"You seem content," Abby said to Duncan.

He gazed out over the expanse of sparkling blue
sea. "I am, lassie. Do ye remember what the Good
Book says about those who're lonely?"

Abby shook her head as she noticed Luke perking
up with interest at their conversation.

"It says God sets the lonely in families." Duncan
twirled his handlebar moustache, a sure sign his
emotions were involved. "I'm thankful He's done
that fer me."

Abby nodded. "I'm thankful He's done that for
all of us," she said, thinking of the reunion that
would soon take place with Ma, Pa, and Uncle
Samuel. She continued with her pencil sketch,
capturing the new grin that was spreading across
Luke's freckled face.

When he winked at her with one mischievous green eye, she knew Luke was thinking not only of the Kendalls, but also that he was now part of God's forever family.

Abby smiled and penciled in a thought below his picture: "With God all things are possible."

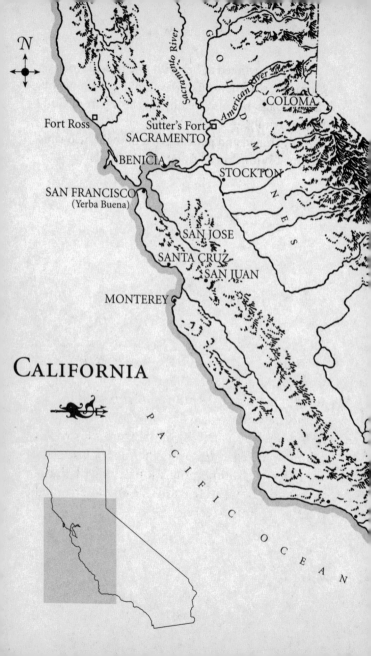

*Don't miss the next exciting adventure in
the South Seas Adventures series:*

Abby
Secret at
Cutter Grove

When the Kendalls and friends travel to Kauai
to investigate the sugar business, Abby's
excited. After all, that island's the perfect spot
to search for clues about what happened to
Duncan's father—missing now for over thirty
years. But upon arriving at the Cutter Grove
Plantation, Abby discovers the sugar business
isn't all sweet. Something's sour at the plantation, and Abby and friend Luke are determined
to unravel the mystery.

Hawaiian People, Places, and Words

Follow these two simple rules to say Hawaiian words correctly:

1. Don't end a syllable with a consonant. For example, Honolulu should be pronounced Ho-no-lu-lu, not Hon-o-lu-lu.

2. Say each vowel in a word. The vowels generally are pronounced like this:
   a as in daughter
   e as in prey
   i as in ring
   o as in cold
   oo as in tool

aloha—word of welcome or farewell, a type of unconditional love shared

kahuna—a priest of the Hawaiian religion, or a holy or wise man

kanaka—Hawaiian man or worker

Lanai—small island near Maui and Molokai

mahalo—thank you

Oahu—a large island in the Hawaiian chain, where Honolulu is located

Nautical Words

bark—a small sailing ship

bow—the front of a ship

dinghy—a small boat

gunwale—the upper edge of a ship's side

hatch—a door in the deck of a ship

hull—the frame of a ship

mast—wooden beam that holds up the sails

schooner—a sailing vessel with at least two masts

Spanish Words

amigo—friend

caballeros—horsemen

Californio—original Spanish colonist

Sí estas tu—Yes, is it you?

gracias—thank you

niña—girl

niño—boy

quesadilla—a tortilla filled with meat, cheese, and/
or vegetables; fried; and topped with cheese

Señora—Mrs.

sí—yes

tortilla—round thin bread

vaqueros—cowboys

About the Author

Pamela Walls, a freelance writer and reporter, traveled to the California goldfields to research this Abby book. Standing on the site of Sutter's Mill, where gold was discovered 150 years ago, she dipped her pan in the river and "washed sand."

"It's a lot harder than it looks!" she says. Although she didn't find gold at that overmined site, she did come away with a "minuscule fleck of gold dust in a tiny glass vial that only cost two dollars at the local store."

"But the real treasure I discovered is our nation's history and the colorful characters that risked life and limb to come west," she explains.

At the beginning of the gold rush, the yellow rocks were everywhere. One man pulled up a bush and found a fortune in gold nuggets clinging to the roots. Another was cleaning his gun when it misfired and the bullet hit a distant rock, cracking it open to reveal a rich vein of pure gold.

"Probably the smartest people of all were the ones who supplied food and other items to the thousands of miners who arrived. One woman made eighteen thousand dollars by baking pies. Others made their fortunes through washing laundry or running tent hotels."

Within this work of fiction are many true facts—some of them so far-fetched they might be difficult to believe. While many people lost their lives in the hard living of the 1848-1858 gold rush, many others saw their wildest dreams come true.

"And who knows?" Pamela says with a gleam in her eye. "There could be another rich vein of gold hidden along some creek bed, still waiting to be discovered. But in the meantime, there is one sure way to strike gold now: crack open the Bible and delve into God's promises. It's one treasure you can never use up."

> *"For I know the plans I have for you,"* declares the LORD, *"plans to prosper you and not to harm you, plans to give you hope and a future."* Jeremiah 29:11